Book Clubs Can Be Fatal – A Senior Sleuthing Club Cozy Mystery – Book 1

by

Jinty James

Book Clubs Can Be Fatal – A Senior Sleuthing Club Cozy Mystery – Book 1

by

Jinty James

ISBN:9798399858760

DEDICATION

To my wonderful Mother, Annie, and
AJ.

CHAPTER 1

Prudence Armstrong took a deep breath and knocked on the front door. The yellow and cream Victorian duplex looked well cared for, and the street was quiet. That was a positive sign, because peace and quiet was one of her favorite things. Maybe that's why she became a librarian – technically assistant librarian – because she liked everything to be in order.

And books. She loved books.

"Ruff! Ruff!" came from inside the house.

"Hold your horses, Teddy." She heard a woman's voice. "I'm coming."

"Ruff!" The door swung inward, and Pru stared at a small white bundle of fluff jiggling on the doorstep, his – or her – tail wagging.

"Can I help you?" A senior with curly gray hair springing around her face peered at her. She gripped the handles of her black rolling walker and looked at Pru enquiringly.

"Your friend Noreen said you might be looking for a roommate," Pru blurted out. She'd composed a little speech and had practiced it on the short drive over from the library. But instead, she'd just uttered the first words that had popped into her head.

"Who are you?" The woman frowned.

"Ruff?"

"I'm Pru Armstrong, the assistant librarian at the Gold Leaf Valley library."

"I go to the library all the time and I haven't seen you before." The woman grabbed the front door, as if she were about to shut it in Pru's face.

Buzz. Buzz.

"Drat, that's my phone." The woman felt around the pockets in her pink sweatpants.

"Ruff?" The cute dog reached up a paw and patted the underside of the walker seat.

"Is it in here?" She flipped open the black vinyl padded seat. "Yeah! Good boy, Teddy."

Teddy sat on his haunches, looking pleased.

"Noreen?" The woman spoke on the phone. "Is that you? I've got someone here right now, a girl who says she wants to be roomies with me – you did? But I haven't seen her at the library before – she's brand new?"

Pru shifted slightly as the woman eyed her thoughtfully, all the while talking to her friend on the phone.

Teddy looked at her curiously, and apparently decided she was okay. He put out a paw toward her.

"Hi." Pru squatted and stuck out a tentative hand, noticing his pink collar. "Nice to meet you."

"Ruff." *Hi,* Teddy answered quietly.

She touched his paw – the fur thick and soft, like cotton.

"Okay, Noreen, I'll check her out." The woman ended the call and glanced down at Pru. "Well, it's a good sign Teddy likes you. Noreen told me I should consider having you as a roommate. But first, do you have any ID?"

"Of course." She rose and rummaged around in her large blue purse, pulled out her matching wallet, and showed her driver's license.

"Huh. This says you're from Colorado. So why'd you move down here?" She peered at Pru. "A nice-looking girl like you burying yourself in a small town like this? If I had your auburn hair and cute face, I wouldn't be moving in *here*."

"This is my first job as assistant librarian," Pru replied. "I applied to a lot of libraries, and this is the only job offer I received."

"So you took it." She nodded in approval. "Smart girl. Okay, you can come in and we can have a chat and see if we get on. But I gotta warn you, I've got Lauren, Annie, and Zoe on speed dial, as well as the head detective at the police department. Because he's married to Lauren," she added, closing the front door behind Pru.

"Lauren, Annie, and Zoe?" Pru asked faintly, wondering if she'd done the right thing by knocking on this woman's door. But her only other housing option was staying at the local motel – and although Paul, the owner, had given her a discounted rate, it was adding up fast. And she missed home cooked food already. Although, he made a pretty tasty breakfast of bacon and eggs, or pancakes, and didn't charge extra.

"My pals. I'm Martha, by the way." Martha turned and stuck out her hand.

"Pru," she introduced herself again, noting how strong the handshake was for a woman who she guessed to be in her seventies.

"Let's talk in the living room." Martha trundled through the cream painted hall, Teddy running ahead.

"So why do you want to be roomies with me?" Martha plonked herself down on the comfortable looking yellow sofa, waving a hand at the opposite couch. Teddy clambered up

5

beside her and looked at Pru enquiringly.

"Because there's nowhere else to live." She decided to be honest. Sitting down on the opposite two-seater, she clutched her purse on her lap. "Noreen came into the library and heard me asking Barbara, my boss, about housing and came up to us and said her friend Martha might be looking for a roommate because she got a dog." She furrowed her brow.

"Noreen was right." Martha gently stroked Teddy. "See, I've only had this little guy for a month – got him from the shelter – and went a bit overboard with my spending. Do you know how much fancy dog beds, toys, food, and collars cost? I thought it would be fun if his collars matched my outfits—" she pointed to her pink sweatshirt and pants, and then at Teddy's collar "—but didn't realize until I got my credit card bill how much it ended up costing me." She turned to Teddy. "But you're worth it, aren't you little guy?"

"Ruff!"

"So I was talking to Noreen about how I might have to get a roomie for a while to help make ends meet, since I'm on a fixed income, and she said it was a good idea. And now you're suddenly here on the doorstep!" Martha grinned. "I only spoke to her about it two days ago."

"And Noreen told me this morning. I came over as soon as my shift finished."

"I guess we can give it a go." Martha looked at her consideringly. "I've got a guest bedroom you can use and a bathroom down the hall. I have my own bathroom, so we won't disturb each other that way."

"Thank you." She inhaled a small breath of relief.

"Now, how much should I charge you?" Martha wrinkled her brow. "Hmm. I think six hundred would be fair, don't you? That's per month, and one month in advance."

"I can afford that." She pulled out her wallet, and counted out the cash. She wouldn't have much left after she paid her motel bill until she received her first paycheck, but it would be worth it.

"Thanks." Martha recounted the wad of notes. "Not that I don't trust you, but my mom always taught me to count everything myself."

"So did mine." She smiled at Martha, who beamed back.

"Well, let's get you settled in."

"Ruff!" Teddy jumped off the couch and ran over to Pru, planting his paws on her knees.

"He's saying welcome." Martha chuckled.

"I'll drive over to the motel and grab my things." She patted the dog, then rose.

"We'll be here," Martha said cheerfully.

"Ruff!" *Yes!*

***

"You haven't got much." Martha eyed the two tan suitcases in the hallway.

"It's pretty much all I need," Pru replied a little defensively. Apart from books. Most of her treasures were still in her bedroom at home – her *childhood* home, she supposed she should call it now. *This* was her new home.

"I'll give you the tour." Martha wheeled her and Teddy toward the living room. "You've already been in here, but the kitchen's through there—" she waved a hand toward the rear of the room, "—and you can get to the backyard through it. But be careful if you go on the lawn because I haven't picked up all of Teddy's business yet."

"I can do that," she replied, wanting to be helpful.

"Goody!" Martha's face lit up.

"Ruff!" Teddy looked at Pru in approval.

"Your bedroom is here." Martha wheeled herself around and trundled toward the hall. And the bathroom is here. My bedroom is over there."

Martha opened the door to the guest bedroom decorated in tones of cream and beige. "It's a bit boring – sorry. Oops–" she whizzed over to the bed and swept a couple of sweatpants onto her walker seat. "I forgot I left them in here. I was sorting out some of my clothes – a while ago."

Pru placed her suitcases on the double bed, covered with a slightly garish orange bedspread.

"I thought that color would cheer things up in here, but I don't think it worked."

"I don't mind," she replied. And right now, she didn't. She was just glad she had a comfortable place to live. And company – although she wasn't quite sure what to make of Martha yet.

"Lemme check the closet." Martha opened the cream closet door, a slight creak emitting. "Oh yeah, I forgot about this stuff, too." She pulled two jogger suits off the hangers and tossed them onto the walker. "So that's where my blanket went to!" She brandished a tatty red rug.

"Ruff!" Teddy stretched up on his hind legs, patting the woolen throw with his front paws.

"Do you want it?" Martha played peek-a-boo for a moment, hiding her face behind the blanket, then popping out at Teddy.

"Ruff!" *Yes!*

"This will keep him nice and warm," Martha declared, "although I've already bought him lots of blankets."

"Where does he sleep?" Pru asked, placing her pajamas under her pillow.

"With me. Or in the living room. Wherever he wants. But mostly with me."

"That's nice." Pru nodded.

"You'll be okay if he wants to visit you during the night, won't you?"

"Yes. I had a dog growing up. He used to sleep on my feet."

"I hope he wasn't too heavy," Martha joked.

"He was sometimes, but I didn't have the heart to move him. He looked so peaceful."

"I knew there was a reason Teddy took a liking to you." Martha grinned.

Pru finished unpacking her clothes.

"You're neat." Martha sounded approving, sitting on the seat of her walker and watching. "That's good. Because I can be messy."

"Ruff!"

"But you're not messy, little guy." Martha beamed at Teddy. "Want to go to the café tomorrow and visit Annie?"

"Ruff!" *Yes!*

"Want to come?" Martha asked her. "Or are you working tomorrow?"

"My shift starts at nine and I finish at five," Pru answered.

"That's a long day." Martha wrinkled her nose. "I'm glad I'm retired now."

"What did you do?" she asked.

"I was a secretary years ago," Martha replied, "but I prefer being retired. I go to the senior center a lot and catch up on all the gossip, and I visit Annie and the girls at the café. Lauren makes the best cupcakes, and Zoe is a hoot! And Annie, who's a Norwegian Forest Cat, seats the customers."

"But I thought you said Annie was a cat." Pru stared at Martha.

"Annie shows customers to a table she picks out for them herself," Martha said proudly. "If you're real lucky, she'll sit with you for a while and talk to you."

"But cats can't talk – unless they meow." She sank down onto the bed.

"Annie can – can't she, Teddy?" She winked at him.

"Ruff!" *Yes!*

"Norwegian Forest Cats have a special way of talking. I thought you'd know that, since you're a librarian." Martha tsked. "Aren't you supposed to know practically everything?"

"I do know a lot of things," Pru replied. "But there are many different cat – and dog – breeds out there. I don't know how each particular breed of cat actually speaks."

"Hmm – fair enough," Martha conceded. "And I didn't know that about Norwegian Forest Cats until I met Annie, anyway." She stood and gripped the handles of her walker. "Want to have dinner together? I guess we should work out what we're going to do grocery-wise. I think when Lauren and Zoe were roomies they split everything half and half."

"That sounds fine to me," she replied.

"I made some chicken soup. There should be enough for both of us."

"Thanks." She smiled.

"You haven't tasted it yet." Martha chuckled. "But it's pretty good, if I do say so myself. Hey, on another night we could get pizza delivered. That's what Lauren and Zoe do, but a big pizza is too much for me and it just doesn't taste the same if you reheat it the next day."

"I like pizza," Pru told her.

"Goody." Martha beamed at her.

She felt like she'd just passed some kind of test.

"Okay, let's heat up the soup." Martha led the way to the kitchen.

Pru offered to help, but she was waved away.

"I can do it." Martha puttered about the small kitchen. "You can sit over there—" she pointed to a four-seater dining table nearby "—and tell me more about yourself."

"Well, there's not much to tell," Pru replied cautiously. "I got my library degree in Colorado, and sent out my resume and applied to every library job I found, and I have two older brothers."

"I don't know why you didn't get more job offers," Martha mused, stirring the soup. A savory chicken aroma wafted from the saucepan. "But it's lucky for me you didn't." She turned and beamed at Pru.

Pru found herself smiling back.

Over the delicious chicken soup, which Martha said was her secret recipe and she would never tell what was in it, Pru mentioned having to organize a book club at the library.

"My boss asked me to set it up." She spooned up some more broth.

"That sounds like fun!"

"Ruff!" Teddy sat at the table with them, on a chair next to Martha. When Pru had glanced at him in surprise, Martha told her that Annie had taught him how to do it.

"Would you like to come?" Pru asked. "I'm worried I won't get enough people and the patron who's been asking my boss about it will be upset at the small turnout."

"Who wants a book club?"

"A woman called Candy. My boss said she's too busy to deal with it but she's tired of Candy bugging her about it. Those were her exact words."

"Huh. Okay, I'll come," Martha decided. "Because I think roomies should help each other out. But I hope it's not a boring book because then I probably won't read it. It's not a gritty western, is it?"

"No." Pru looked at her in puzzlement. "It's a women's fiction novel."

"What's that?"

"It's … it's about a woman, or sometimes more than one, and something happens in their lives which makes them discover something about themselves. I think," she added cautiously. "I've only read a couple."

"Does it have romance in it? I like a little romance. Hey, have you seen those princess movies on TV?"

"I've heard of them, but I don't think I've—"

"You've gotta watch them. Doesn't she, Teddy?"

"Ruff!" *Yes!*

"Teddy's watched all three," Martha said proudly. "And I'm working on a fourth. But there might be a problem with that, because now my agent says she can't sell it."

"You've got an agent? You're a screenwriter?" Pru stared at her in astonishment.

"It's like this ..." Martha launched into a long and slightly convoluted tale, but by the end of it Pru understood that Zoe from the café had written the third princess movie and introduced her agent to Martha, and now Martha was working on a TV script as well.

"Maybe you can help me." Martha's eyes lit up. "See, I've got this retired lady detective who's outsmarting these two detective hotshots. I was

17

stuck for a while when she was stranded on a deserted road, but I've got her out of there finally, but now she needs to put those two not-so-hot shot detectives in their place."

"You're not a retired detective in real life, are you?" Pru joked, wondering just who her new roommate was.

"I wish I was!" Martha chuckled. "It would be a hoot to put away the bad guys – although I nearly have a few times now. Lauren, Annie, and Zoe do it all the time."

"They do? I thought Gold Leaf Valley was a safe place to live."

"It is – apart from the occasional bad guy – or girl."

"Oh," she replied faintly.

"You'll see," Martha said in a comforting way, although it didn't sound very comforting to Pru.

CHAPTER 2

Two days later, Pru surveyed the small corner of the library that had been set aside for the new book club. She'd rearranged the comfortable chairs into a circle, with a small table in the center.

"Where is everyone? I'm Candy." A woman with frosted blonde hair and pink lipstick bustled up to her. She wore a pink pants suit with a white blouse, and pink high-heel shoes.

"I'm sure they'll be here in a minute," Pru replied, hoping that was the truth. Martha had promised she'd be there, but she hadn't caught sight of her roommate yet.

"It's supposed to start in three minutes." The woman glanced at her watch encrusted with sparkling stones.

"Perhaps you'd like to take a seat," she invited.

Candy looked around the room, seeming to take in the rows of bookcases, the children's corner, the nonfiction area with tables and chairs, and the computer corner, where patrons could access the internet for free.

"Don't we need some more chairs? I'm sure more than seven people will show up."

"I can grab more chairs if we need them," Pru replied.

Candy sighed. "I guess this will have to do." She made it sound like that would be a big effort. "You do have enough copies of the book for everyone, don't you?"

"Yes." She nodded. "We've bought ten copies."

"Good." Candy sounded pleased.

Pru glanced around the large room. Barbara, her boss, was busy at the reference desk helping a patron find a book about particular types of mushrooms.

A few patrons wandered among the shelves, a girl in her late teens chuckling happily as she scooped up a book from the mystery shelf.

A cell phone rang, and Barbara looked up and shushed the offending owner, who blushed and hastily turned off the sound. Pru knew from her work experience in previous libraries that some librarians were more tolerant of ring tones and people talking in loud voices, but she was glad that her boss wasn't. If that made her old-fashioned, she didn't mind.

"Is this book club?" A tall, thin, middle-aged woman wearing a fawn skirt and sweater walked over to them. "I hope I'm not late."

"Not at all," Pru greeted her, a tiny sigh of relief leaving her shoulders at seeing someone turn up.

"I'm Ms. Tobin," the woman said.

"I'm Pru, the assistant librarian, and this is Candy."

"Hello." Ms. Tobin nodded and smiled at both of them.

"Let's sit down." Candy gestured to Ms. Tobin to take a seat in one of the comfortable beige chairs, and sat next to her, placing her pink and white tote bag on the carpet.

A man with gray hair who looked to be in his early seventies tentatively approached.

"Hi, are you here for book club?" Pru greeted him.

"Yes." He looked relieved to be in the right place.

"Take a seat." She waved a hand at the empty chairs. "We should be getting started in a few minutes." She hoped.

She noticed Ms. Tobin speaking to the man briefly as he sat down next to Candy.

Pru realized she hadn't gotten the books and hurried over to the desk. There they were, replete with a cover of a blonde woman running towards the sunset and the title, *Race to the Sunset.*

"I'm looking for the new book club." An elegant woman in her late forties strode up to the desk. She wore a smart beige suit and carried a classic purse decorated with three metal buckles.

"It's right over there." Pru nodded toward the corner. "I'm just collecting the books for everyone."

"Good." The woman smiled briefly.

Pru watched her join the others. Where was Martha? Was she coming?

"Has it started?" A woman rushed up to her, pushing a strand of limp hair off her brow. She wore jeans and a slightly dusty green sweater.

"Not yet. Everyone's getting settled over there." Pru gestured to the small gathering.

"Thanks." The woman dashed over to the circle and plunked herself down.

"Yoo-hoo, Pru! Here I am!" Martha charged toward her, fingers clenched on her rolling walker handles. "Not late, am I?"

"No." Pru smiled, noticing her roommate wore turquoise sweatpants and a matching sweater.

"Goody." Martha's eyes lit up as she noticed the small group. "Ms. Tobin's here!"

"You know her?"

"Oh, yeah." Martha nodded. "She's one of Annie's regulars. I don't know the others, though – but I think that gal works at Gary's Burger Diner."

"Which—"

But Martha was already racing over to the comfy corner.

"Well, I guess everyone is here." Pru came over to them, holding a stack of books. "Hello. My name is Pru and I'm the assistant librarian." She still got a thrill saying that and wondered if the novelty would ever wear off – although her goal was to become a library director one day.

"Perhaps everyone could introduce themselves, and then we can start talking about this book." She handed out the copies – Candy practically snatched hers and started flicking through it.

Ms. Tobin introduced herself, then Candy said importantly, "I'm Candy, and this book club was my idea. I think this author, Becky Blanche, is absolutely wonderful, and I wanted to share her books with everyone."

"I'm Eleanor," the elegant woman said, glancing at Candy.

"My name is Hal and I haven't read this author before – or many lady authors." The gray-haired man glanced down at the book in his hands. "My wife said I should read something about women, so I guess here I am."

Everyone chuckled.

"I'm Doris, and I haven't read a book for years." The woman in the green sweater chewed her lip. "I thought it would be good for me to try something different."

"Wonderful." Ms. Tobin nodded in approval.

"I know you." Martha pointed a finger at Doris. "You work at Gary's Burger Diner. They have the best burgers. Especially the smoky barbecue special." She looked over at Pru. "We should go there one day."

"Do you two know each other?" Ms. Tobin asked.

"She's my new roomie." Martha grinned.

"Ruff!" A faint noise sounded from the walker basket.

Pru stared at Martha, and then at the walker. The black vinyl that comprised the basket moved slightly.

"You don't have—"

"Ruff!" Teddy's head poked out of the basket, pushing up the seat.

"That's a dog!" Eleanor paled.

"He wanted to come," Martha said, a little apologetically. "I told him I wasn't sure if animals were allowed in the library but he looked so sad to be left home alone that I had to bring him. He's used to coming to the café with me."

"That's true." Ms. Tobin nodded. "Lauren doesn't have a problem with him being there, and he and Annie are good company for each other."

"Oh, is that Annie's café?" Doris asked. "I'm usually working a shift when they're open."

"That's the one." Martha grinned. "I'm gonna take Pru to meet them when she has some free time."

"How lovely." Ms. Tobin smiled. "You're in for a treat, dear," she told Pru.

"Can we get back to this book?" Candy tapped the cover with a pink fingernail.

"But what about the dog?" Eleanor asked. She turned to Pru. "Are dogs allowed in this library?"

"Is he a service dog?" Pru asked hopefully. She hadn't seen Teddy wear a special vest, but she also hadn't seen him out and about with Martha.

"No." Martha's mouth turned upside down. "I've only had him a month, and he's only seven months old. He's still growing up."

"If he's not a service dog, he shouldn't be in this building," Eleanor said primly.

Pru glanced over at her boss, still engrossed in her conversation about mushrooms with the patron. It seemed she hadn't heard Teddy announce his presence.

"But he's so cute," Doris said. "Can't he stay?"

"He's not bothering me," Hal put in.

"Yeah, he'll be good. He promises, don't cha, little guy?" Martha looked down at the white bundle of fluff.

"Ruff," he said quietly. *Yes.*

"Well …" Eleanor hesitated. "I suppose. But only for today. I don't expect him to be here next week," she told Martha.

"Okay." Martha nodded. "Thanks."

"Now we've got that out of the way, we need to talk about this book," Candy said insistently.

"Why don't you start?" Pru suggested, wondering why she was so persistent about this particular novel. Did Candy really love the author so much? Although, *she* loved reading a lot of authors, so perhaps she shouldn't criticize.

"*Race to the Sunset*," Candy said, holding up the book like a game show hostess, "is simply marvelous. It's about a woman who is in search of meaning, and moves to the beach, where she meets the love of her life, along with an interesting old lady who recounts her own love story."

Eleanor stared at Candy. "Really?"

"Yes, really," Candy assured her. "The heroine also discovers she has an affinity for water and swims in the ocean every day, even during rough and stormy weather."

"Doesn't she drown?" Martha asked.

"Of course not!" Candy frowned. "The hero rescues her."

"Oh," Doris said. "But I thought this was women's fiction and not romance. But maybe I'm wrong."

"Yes, you are wrong," Candy assured her loftily. "Women's fiction can have romance in it but not technically be known as a romance novel. It might be boring if there's no romance at all."

"Yes, it might be," Eleanor said in a faintly sarcastic tone.

"Huh," Martha muttered.

"Why don't we turn to page one?" Candy suggested, doing so. "I'll start reading it out for everyone.
'*Melisande walked along the sand, the crunch echoing in her toes. She almost tripped over a large rock, but*

neatly righted herself. Shading her eyes with her hand, she looked out over the ocean, marveling at the majestic waves rolling into shore. When she—' "

"When does she meet the guy?" Martha interrupted. "Is he a hottie? I hope so, otherwise it *will* be boring."

"Yes, he's a hottie," Candy replied crisply, "although I prefer the term handsome."

"What about the old woman?" Eleanor asked. "When does she appear?"

"Later on," Candy replied. "Now, where was I? Oh yes, '*When she found a seashell, she bent down to pick it up. Suddenly, she found herself noticing—' "*

"The hottie!" Martha chortled. "I bet she sees his feet standing right there and she blushes and then—"

"No, that does not happen," Candy said severely.

"Oh." Doris sounded disappointed.

"What if everyone starts reading silently to themselves?" Pru suggested. "We could all read chapter one and then discuss it. We should have time." She glanced at the big white clock on the wall. Still forty minutes to go.

"All right," Candy replied with a sigh.

The sound of pages turning filled the room as the seven of them, including Pru, read the first chapter. When she finished first, the speed-reading course she'd taken in college coming in handy, she looked around the little group. Teddy had fallen asleep in the walker basket, looking as cute as could be, while Martha shuffled the pages, frowning.

Doris read slowly, using a finger. When she noticed Pru watching, she blushed, but Pru nodded encouragingly. After all, she used a finger for speed reading which really helped.

When Ms. Tobin looked up expectantly, along with Eleanor, Pru cleared her throat.

"Is everyone just about finished?" she asked.

"I've got one more page," Hal said.

"I've got two." Martha tapped her open page. "I don't get it."

"What don't you get?" Candy asked.

"The whole story. So far she's just walking along the beach and there's no guy or anything happening."

"That's because the scene is being set," Candy told her.

"Well, I don't like it," Martha replied. "Sorry. I need to read something where there's action right away. Or else it's funny right away."

"Maybe we should read chapter two," Ms. Tobin suggested.

"Good idea." Candy nodded.

"Okay." Martha sighed. She flipped a couple of pages and started reading.

Teddy continued to doze in the basket, twitching a little, his eyes closed.

Everyone started reading chapter two, Pru included. She hoped the story improved. Sneaking a glance at the big wall clock, she sighed silently when she noticed there were still nearly twenty-five minutes to go.

At the end of chapter two, Melisande was still strolling along the beach. Pru couldn't help wondering when she took a dip in the ocean. No sign of the romantic male lead, either.

"So," Pru took a deep breath, "what does everyone think about chapter two?"

"I've still got three pages to go," Hal said apologetically. He scratched his thinning scalp. "Is this what my wife wanted me to read? A lady strolling along the beach?"

"Maybe I shouldn't have tried reading this book," Doris admitted, looking downhearted. "I don't get it, either. Maybe books aren't for me."

"Don't say that," Pru replied, dismayed. "I can help you choose another book afterward, if you like. Maybe you'll find another genre more to your taste."

"Yeah, like something funny," Martha added. "Hey, are there any books like those princess movies?" She turned to Doris. "You were at Zoe's premiere, right? For the third movie?"

"I was." Doris smiled. "I love those films."

"There you go." Martha pointed her finger at Pru. "Find Doris a book like that."

"No problem." Pru smiled at both of them. "It will be my pleasure."

"Thanks." Doris looked pleased.

"Ahem. If we can get back to this book," Candy directed. "Now let's discuss the first two chapters. Melisande is doing some important musing about her life while she's strolling along the windswept beach. She's about to decide to brave the chilly depths of the ocean because although there are a lot of waves, there is just something about them that compels her to—"

"How do you know that?" Hal interrupted. "Have you read this book before?"

"Yes, I have – more than once – because that's how good it is," Candy replied loftily. "If you remember, I did mention at the beginning how much I love this author and how I want more people to know about her. These books are amazing! The library had to order these copies because they didn't have any books by her at all." Candy shook her head, as if not able to understand such a thing.

"Perhaps the library didn't know about them," Pru suggested gently. She flipped to the copyright page. "They're published by a small press."

"I'm sure this author will be published by a big publishing house one day and her books will be stocked in every library in the country." Candy nodded decisively. "It will just take some time. So the more people who read Becky Blanche, the better."

"Are you organizing any other book clubs?" Eleanor spoke.

"Why, as a matter of fact I am," Candy told her. "I'm organizing one in Sacramento – the librarian there has bought fifteen copies of this book because she expects a much bigger turn out." She glanced around the small circle dismissively. "I don't understand why more people didn't come today."

"Maybe it takes a little time for something new to get going," Pru said.

"Well, anyway." Candy tossed her frosted locks. "I—"

"Pru." Her boss strode over, the severe edges of her dark bob hitting her cheeks. "The French conversation group will be arriving shortly and we need to get their room set up."

Pru cast a hurried look toward Martha's walker, but there was no sign of Teddy. Martha plopped her book on top of the walker seat, slowly moving it down and hiding the puppy in her basket. Only a slight movement in the side of the black basket hinted at Teddy's presence.

"Is that the time already?" Pru's gaze flew to the clock.

"Goody." Martha's eyes brightened. "We can go home now."

"You all need to finish reading the book this week," Candy ordered, "so we can have a proper discussion about it next time."

"I'll try." Hal rose. "My wife will probably make me, anyway."

"Good." Candy nodded.

"I should be able to," Ms. Tobin declared. "It will be a change from reading mysteries, although I love them. Perhaps my cat Miranda will enjoy reading it with me."

Everyone gathered their things and rose. Candy's gaze was hawklike, as if to ensure they each took their copy of the book.

"Doris, I'm sure you'll be able to understand the plot," Candy said, catching the other woman's eye.

"Oh – thanks." Pink polished Doris's cheeks.

"Let me find you a book I think you'll like," Pru told her. "Can you wait a few minutes while I set up the room for the next group?"

"Yeah. My shift starts later this morning, but I have to be at the diner in twenty minutes."

"Why don't you browse the shelves and I'll catch up with you?" Pru suggested, conscious of her boss nearby.

The book club members filed out of the library, checking out their copy of *Race to the Sunset* on the way out. Martha winked at Pru.

She was glad no one in the group had told her boss that Teddy had been there as an unofficial member.

Candy was the last to leave, telling Barbara that she really needed to buy every single book written by Becky Blanche, and that other libraries in California had done so.

"I'll look into it," Barbara promised impatiently.

"Your patrons don't know what they're missing," Candy said, on her way out of the building.

Pru quickly helped set up the small room next door for French conversation – a large, horseshoe shaped table with hard plastic chairs, and a screen adorning one wall.

"Hope I didn't keep you too long." Pru rushed over to Doris, who browsed the mystery shelves.

"That's okay." Doris smiled. "You seem busy."

"I've got plenty of time now to help you. I thought we could take a look at the young adult shelves. Lots of grown-ups read young adult, and there are plenty of books I think you might like if you enjoy the princess movies."

"What about this one?" Doris held out *Aunt Dimity's Death.*

"Oh, I think you'll love this." It had been a few years since she'd read it, but the story came flooding back. "I did."

"You've read it?" Doris looked intrigued.

"I loved it."

"Okay, I'll get it. Thanks. I could try young adult next time."

"Do you have a library card?"

"No." Doris looked panicked.

"No problem. You just have to fill out a form with your information, and then you can check out this book, plus *Race to the Sunset.*"

Pru led her over to the desk, and handed her the short form and a pen. After Doris filled it in, she made up the library card and laminated it.

"You're all set." Pru handed the books over to Doris.

"Thanks." Doris looked down at the two novels. "I really want to start reading this Aunt Dimity one, but I guess I should finish reading the book club novel first."

"Maybe you'll have time to read both by next week?" Pru suggested.

"Maybe." Doris sounded doubtful. "Well, thanks, anyway. See you next week." She walked out of the library, flicking through one of the books – Pru wondered if it was the Aunt Dimity mystery.

After everyone arrived for French conversation, Pru had a few minutes for herself. No one needed her help and there were no books to shelve or to unpack. She decided to look up *Race to the Sunset*. Why was Candy so insistent about everyone reading this novel?

After checking a few websites, Pru frowned. Unless readers were buying the book directly from the small press publisher, the sales were not good at all. She flipped to the copyright page on her own copy. It was published a few months ago. Hmm.

After her lunchbreak, the afternoon was busy and the time flew by. When she arrived home at Martha's duplex, all she wanted to do was relax and see if Teddy wanted her to play with him. But Martha had other ideas.

CHAPTER 3

"Hope you're hungry." Martha grinned at her. She and Teddy sat on the sofa, looking at a menu. "It's pizza night!"

"It is?" Pru flopped on the opposite sofa.

"Yeah – remember we talked about it? Now, I'm wondering if we should get a half and half. See, I really want to try the Lauren special, but the Zoe special sounds good, too. But two pizzas will probably be too much for us – plus it will cost double. How much do you eat?" Martha peered at her inquisitively from the other couch.

"A normal amount?"

"Yeah, me too." Martha chuckled. "I guess we should order just one, and then if we're still hungry, we can fill up on ice cream. I've got salted caramel in the freezer."

"That sounds good," Pru replied. "Wait a minute – did you say a

Lauren special and a Zoe special? You mean the girls from the café? Do they make pizza too?"

"No, they just order it so much – well they used to – that the owner decided to name two pizzas in their honor. Hey! If we start ordering tons of pizza, maybe he'll do the same for us! Or—" Martha's eyes widened as she glanced at her dog, "—a Teddy pizza!"

"Ruff!" *Yes!*

"That's a … really interesting idea," Pru replied.

"Isn't it?" Martha grinned. "Okay, so I'll order us one. Are you hungry now?" She looked at her hopefully.

"Yes," she surprised herself by answering. It was barely six but she realized how much she was looking forward to her dinner.

"Goody." Martha picked up her phone from the coffee table and stabbed the buttons. When she ended the call, she said, "That's seven dollars each."

"Oh." Pru reached into her purse and found the correct money. "Here you go."

"Thanks. So what do you think of that book we have to read?" Martha wrinkled her nose. "I don't think I'm gonna make it through the whole thing."

"You're not?"

"Don't think it's my cup of tea – or hot chocolate. But I was thinking, after pizza you could help me with my TV script. Remember, I'm a bit stuck now I've got my retired lady detective out of that deserted stretch of road and—"

A knock sounded at the front door.

"I'll go." Pru grabbed the money and hurried to answer it, her stomach growling.

The young delivery guy grinned at her and handed her the pizza. "Enjoy."

"We sure will," Martha called out after him. "Yum. And by ordering today, we got the senior discount."

The tempting aroma of red sauce, melted cheese, and – was that pepperoni? – teased her senses.

"You didn't tell me exactly what's on this pizza." Pru lifted the lid, her eyes widening.

"Only good stuff." Martha clambered to her feet. "Okay, let's start eating."

They sat at the kitchen table, Teddy by Martha's feet, watching hopefully for scraps.

"Pepperoni isn't good for dogs," she warned Martha.

"Pooh. Because I bet he would like some. Sorry, little guy." Martha looked down at the puppy. We've got to be good. You don't want to get sick."

"Ruff." *No.*

Pru dug into her slice of the Lauren special – Canadian bacon, mushroom, and sundried tomato, while Martha ate her piece of pepperoni and sausage.

"So," Martha finished chewing her slice, "I thought you could read this book for me and then tell me what happens, like a book report."

Pru put down her knife and fork and stared at her. "But the whole point of book club is to read the book yourself so you have that experience, and so you can discuss it with the others."

"Yeah, but I bet no one will know if I cheated." Martha grinned.

"I will."

"Ruff!"

"O-kay." Martha sighed. "It was worth a try. Plus, I noticed how fast you were reading those first two chapters, with your finger."

"I learned speed reading in college so I could finish my required reading faster."

"Smart girl." Martha grinned. "Have you got any other hobbies? I like doing water color painting at the senior center. That one's mine." She pointed to a blue and muddy brown picture on the wall.

Pru squinted, trying to work out what it depicted.

"It's the creek by the park," Martha explained.

"Oh, yes," she tried to sound encouraging, although she hadn't visited the local park yet.

"I know it's not that great but I had fun doing it. And it's good for me to catch up with everyone down there and make sure I don't miss out on any gossip."

"Ruff!" Teddy agreed.

"This little guy isn't allowed in, though." Martha pouted. "So I don't like leaving him home alone too long."

"I understand." She nodded.

They finished their pizza in companiable silence. "So, what do you think about helping me with my TV script?" Martha launched into the story about her retired lady detective again, telling Pru exactly where she was stuck.

She tried to stop a yawn from escaping. Martha's script sounded interesting, but it had been a long day and she had to get up early tomorrow.

"You can think about it tonight," Martha suggested. "Lemme know tomorrow if you come up with an idea."

"I will."

"Ruff!"

***

One week later, Pru found herself looking forward to book club that morning. She'd finished reading *Race to the Sunset*, and had noticed Martha wading through it reluctantly.

"I've got five pages to go." Martha mumbled through a mouthful of raisin toast. "Got any more ideas for my TV script?"

"Not since last week." She'd come up with a prank pizza delivery order, inspired by their pizza night, which Martha proclaimed was genius, but nothing since.

"That's great you've nearly finished the book," she encouraged.

"Yeah, I guess." Martha made a moue. "Since someone wouldn't read it for me." Then she smiled. "Just kidding. I guess it's a good thing you didn't do my homework for me."

Pru drew in a slight breath, but didn't think her roommate noticed. "Yes, it is," she said after a moment. "Well, I've got to go to work. See you in a couple of hours."

"You betcha."

"Ruff!" Teddy sat next to Martha, peering at the open book.

"Maybe I should have got Teddy to read it for me," Martha joked.

***

At five minutes to ten, the book club members started arriving.

"Hi," Doris said, waving two books. "I finished Aunt Dimity. I loved it! Do you have the second one?"

"We should have," Pru replied, glad to see the spark of book love in Doris's eye. "If we don't, I can hunt it down for you."

"That would be great." Doris handed the cozy mystery to her. "Do I give it to you? Or is there somewhere I'm supposed to put it?"

"Giving it to me is fine," Pru assured her. "But you can also put it on the returns desk over there." She gestured to the library desk behind them.

"Oh. Sorry."

"No worries." Pru quickly placed the book on the desk and rejoined her. "How did you go with *Race to the Sunset*?"

"Not great." Doris wrinkled her nose. "I'm glad I read the Aunt Dimity first because otherwise I'd start to think I was a big dummy not liking this book. I found it hard to get through." She looked down at the cover of the blonde woman running toward the sunset.

"This wouldn't be my first choice either," Pru confided, feeling slightly guilty, since Candy was also a patron, "but it's good to experiment with different kinds of genres – and authors."

"Do you think Martha will bring her puppy today? He's so cute."

"I hope not." She clapped a hand to her mouth as soon as she heard her own words. "I'm sorry. I love the little guy already, but I don't want Martha to get in trouble if my boss Barbara finds out about him." And she didn't want to get in trouble, either. She needed this job.

"I understand." Doris nodded. "I'd love to have my own dog, but I work different shifts and when it's crazy busy at the diner I'm asked to do overtime." Noticing the concerned look on Pru's face, she continued, "It's okay. Gary is a good boss and pays everyone properly. And everyone shares the tips as well."

"That's good." Pru nodded.

"Hello." Ms. Tobin entered the library, wearing an amber skirt and cream blouse. "I'm not tardy, am I?"

"No, I've just arrived," Doris replied.

"Where is everyone?" Ms. Tobin glanced at the clock on the wall. "Oh, dear, I hope we're not going to be late starting. I wanted to visit the girls at the café after this, before the busy lunch rush."

"I'm sure we'll begin in a few minutes," Pru reassured her. "Did you enjoy reading *Race to the Sunset*?"

"I'm afraid it was not my cup of tea – or coffee." Ms. Tobin frowned. "My little Miranda didn't like it, either. And she enjoyed Agatha Christie."

Pru wasn't quite sure what to say, so she just smiled and gestured for Ms. Tobin to take a seat in the cozy circle.

"I'm here!" Martha raced toward them like a racing car driver. "Finally finished that dratted book – yuck!"

"I'm glad I'm not the only one who didn't enjoy it much," Doris confided. "But I loved the mystery I found. Do you read those, Martha?"

"Sometimes," Martha replied. "Why don't you give it to me and I'll see if Teddy and I like it? He didn't like this one." She made a little face as she glanced down at the cover.

"Neither did my Miranda." Ms. Tobin and Martha started discussing their pets' little foibles.

Pru headed to the returns desk, and scanned the Aunt Dimity cozy, before returning to the circle of chairs and handing it to Martha.

"You can check it out when book club is finished."

"Thanks." Martha studied the cover which featured a pink bunny. "This looks like it might be interesting."

"Oh, it is," Doris said eagerly, and began telling Martha and Ms. Tobin about the plot.

Pru eyed Martha's walker basket but couldn't spot any tell-tale wriggles.

"You didn't bring Teddy, did you?" She kept her voice low so her boss at the reference desk wouldn't overhear.

"You asked me not to, so I didn't," Martha replied. "I tried to explain it to the little guy, so I hope he understood."

"I'm sure he did," Ms. Tobin said. "I swear my little Miranda understands what I tell her, and I'm certain your Teddy does, too. He's such a dear little boy."

"Isn't he?" Martha beamed, and started telling Ms. Tobin about her fur baby's favorite ball.

"Am I late?" Hal arrived, breathing heavily. "My wife told me I had to finish the book before I got here, so I was reading it at breakfast."

"So was I." Martha winked. "And I finished it!"

"Me too." He nodded.

"I wonder where Candy and Eleanor are?" Pru glanced at the time. Five after ten.

"Perhaps we should get started," Ms. Tobin suggested.

"Good idea." Martha nodded. "I promised Teddy we could go to the café after."

"That's where I'm going." Ms. Tobin smiled at her.

"Goody."

"Sorry I'm late." Candy rushed into the library, her pink and white tote bag flapping against her pink dress. She tossed back her frosted locks. "Has everyone read the book? What did you think?"

"Eleanor isn't here," Pru pointed out.

Doris glanced at Candy, her brow crinkled.

"We can start without her," Candy said dismissively. "She mightn't turn up, anyway." She sat down in one of the armchairs. "Now, why don't we discuss the rest of the book? Don't you think it was simply marvelous when Melisande—"

"Have you already started?" Eleanor strode up to the little group. "Someone cut in front of me in the parking lot." She sounded annoyed. "I had to park down the street and walk up."

"We're just about to begin," Pru hoped her tone sounded soothing. Were book clubs always like this? This was her first time hosting one, although she'd assisted when she'd worked temporarily in other libraries while studying.

"Good." Eleanor sat next to Hal and Pru. "I thought it was a simply dreadful book." She shook her head. "I have no idea how it got published."

Candy sucked in a breath. "You don't know what you're talking about! This is a great book! Isn't it?" she demanded, looking at everyone sitting in the circle.

"Umm, it was … different," Doris said.

"It's certainly different to Agatha Christie," Ms. Tobin put in.

"Yeah." Martha nodded vigorously.

"My wife liked it," Hal offered. "That's one of the reasons why I only finished it this morning. Whenever I had some time to read it, it was already in her hands!"

The group chuckled.

"Wonderful!" Candy smiled. "Why don't you ask your wife to join us next week?"

"I suppose she might be interested," he replied. Looking at Pru, he said, "Is there room for one more? Otherwise my wife could have my place."

"I'm sure we could accommodate both of you," she replied quickly, conscious of Candy's narrowing gaze.

"Oh." He sounded disappointed.

"Let's discuss Melisande swimming in the ocean."

Pru found herself losing track of the conversation as Candy enthused about Melisande's new found love of swimming, and instead wondered what book she should read next – when she had time. Definitely some sort of mystery, but which?

"And now, we find out all about the old lady's own romance in the dim, distant past," Candy said.

Pru blinked and straightened up in the chair. She was lucky that her boss expected her to participate in the group, so "everyone could stay on track" so it was like a little work break for her, but that didn't mean she could drift off into her own private book world.

"That was my favorite part," Eleanor said. "So much more interesting than boring Melisande."

"Melisande is not boring!" Candy flashed. "Why, she is this author's best character!"

"If you say so," Eleanor sniped.

"I do!"

"Why don't we discuss the old lady's romance?" Pru tried to get the conversation back on course. "I thought it was interesting when she revealed that she grew up in Italy."

"I love pizza," Martha put in. "Hey! Wouldn't it be something if I went there one day and tried the pizza in Italy? Maybe Teddy could come with me!"

"That does sound interesting," Ms. Tobin said. "But I'd have to leave my Miranda at home with someone looking after her – unless I board her."

"Maybe Lauren and Zoe could start a pet sitting business," Martha joked. "After all, they tried doing a kitty daycare."

"Kitty daycare?" Pru sank back in her armchair and stared at her roommate.

"I wasn't there myself, but I heard it was a real hoot!" Martha chuckled.

"Miranda went to it," Ms. Tobin said, "and I'm sure it gave her a little more confidence."

"People!" Candy clapped her hands. "We are not talking about cats – or dogs. We are talking about the special love story in this book, which is integral to the whole plot. Now, where was I?" She glanced down at her book and flipped a few pages.

"You were somewhere boring. Sorry." Martha looked a little contrite as she realized what she'd said. "But this book just didn't do it for me. Can't we talk about something else?"

"No, we can't," Candy snapped. "We are talking about *Race to the Sunset.* I'm trying to expand your reading horizons. The whole world needs to know just how wonderful Becky Blanche is."

"I don't think any of us think Becky Blanche is a good writer," Eleanor snarked.

"Everyone has different tastes." Pru tried to calm things down, and glanced over at her boss, still engrossed in researching something at the reference desk, thank goodness. "I think we were talking about the old lady's romance in Italy. Why don't we go back to that?"

"Thank you, Pru." Candy nodded. "Yes, the old lady had a marvelous romance last century in Rome. She met a young man called Lorenzo, and they fell in love. But then they were torn apart by their families, who wanted Lorenzo to marry a rich girl. He refused, and they made plans to run away together. But he caught tuberculosis and died on the journey to the US, even though she did her best on the ship to nurse him back to health."

"I thought that was sad," Pru put in.

"Yeah." Martha's mouth turned upside down. "I don't like reading about sad stuff."

"Neither do I," Ms. Tobin agreed.

"But can't you see that her romance represents—"

"I liked Aunt Dimity a lot more," Doris muttered.

"What was that?" Candy cupped an ear behind her head. "Speak up, Doris."

"Nothing." Doris turned pink and looked down at the book in her lap.

"Is there going to be book club next week since we've finished reading this tripe?" Eleanor folded her arms across her chest. "Or was it a two-time deal?"

"It continues next week as far as I know," Pru replied cautiously. She hadn't thought that far ahead.

"But we're reading a different book, right?" Martha caught her eye.

"I hope so," Ms. Tobin said. "I'm sorry, Candy, but this book just isn't for me."

"We could read Aunt Dimity," Doris murmured hopefully.

"I had an Aunt Dimity – no, she was Delores," Hal put in. "Who's Aunt Dimity?"

Doris started telling him about the first book when Candy clapped her hands again.

"Stop it! We are here to talk about this book!" She tapped the cover with a long, pink fingernail. "I insist!"

"But I insist we don't." Eleanor glared at her. "It's a stupid book."

"Why you – you – arggh!" Candy jumped to her feet and stormed out of the library, her pink and white tote bag banging against her hip.

"Did I say something wrong?" Eleanor had a satisfied smile on her lips.

"Oh dear," Ms. Tobin said. "Maybe we were a little harsh."

"If you can't say what you really think about a novel at book club, when can you?" Martha asked.

"But we should try to do it as tactfully as possible," Pru said, staring worriedly after Candy. What was her boss going to say?

"Why don't we try another book for next week?" Ms. Tobin suggested. "Doris has been telling us about this Aunt Dimity book. So why don't we read that instead?"

"I'm in." Martha smiled at Doris. "I've already got my copy."

"Why not?" Eleanor agreed. "It can't be any worse than *Race to the Sunset.*"

"All right." Hal nodded.

"I'll see if there are enough copies here." Pru hurried over to the desk and looked up the title. Thankfully, there were enough listed, and she quickly plucked them off the shelf and checked them out.

"Here you go." She handed them out. "Doris, you've already finished it."

"Yes, and I'm going to read book two next."

"That's wonderful," Ms. Tobin praised. "I'm sure you'll be a bookworm in no time if you keep reading stories that appeal to you."

"Thanks." Doris looked pleased.

All three of them silently started reading *Aunt Dimity's Death* while Pru hunted for book two and found it on the shelf. She gave it to Doris, who eagerly started reading.

Pru wondered if Candy would return once she'd calmed down, but fifteen minutes later, there was still no sign of her.

"I'm afraid it's eleven o'clock," Pru announced.

"Already?" Martha looked at her in surprise. "Doris is right. This is a good story."

"Yes, indeed." Ms. Tobin nodded.

"I like it so far," Hal said.

"It's satisfactory," Eleanor said. "See you all next week. I imagine we'll be discussing this mystery?" She held up her copy.

"Yes," Pru replied.

"Goody." Martha sounded delighted.

They all rose and gathered their things.

"I'll see you at the café," Martha told Ms. Tobin. "I have to go home and collect Teddy first."

"Wonderful." Ms. Tobin nodded.

Hal hurried out of the library, waving goodbye. Eleanor followed, and then Doris, after checking out her cozy.

Ms. Tobin departed, then it was just Martha who was left.

"Maybe I should get another book. I bet I can read two in a week."

"I bet you can," Pru replied with a smile.

"Ooh – what about a lucky dip?" Martha trundled to the mystery shelves, closed her eyes, and stretched out her hand. She blinked, and studied the title - *The Inn at*

Holiday Bay: Clue in the Carriage House by Kathi Daley.

Pru checked it out for her.

"Hey, when do you get a lunch break? You could come with me to the café."

"That *is* an interesting idea." She'd been meaning to check out the coffee shop – Martha had made it sound intriguing – and for the last week she'd been having lunch early. "I'll just have to ask Barbara."

Hurrying over to the reference desk, she checked with her boss who agreed. "But don't take longer than forty-five minutes."

"I won't," she promised.

"We'll have to hustle," Martha said when Pru told her. "First we'll get Teddy, then we'll charge over to the café. Ooh – I know! We can call Lauren and ask her to have our drinks ready. What do you feel like? I love a hot chocolate with lots of marshmallows."

"What kind of food do they have for lunch?"

"Cupcakes. And Danish pastries. Ed makes those. You've gotta try both of those. And paninis. I guess you could eat a panini for lunch."

"That sounds good." Pru walked outside with Martha, who dug her phone out of her walker basket. "What about—"

"Oh, shoot. I can't get a signal." Martha frowned and shook her phone. "Maybe we should go over there." She pointed to the corner of the library.

"Okay." Pru glanced at her watch. "Maybe I could try with my cell."

"Good one." Martha nodded. "But I'll have to give you the number from my phone. Lemme have another go." She put the phone on her walker seat and trundled to the secluded corner of the building. "Uh oh."

"What?" Pru came up behind her and sucked in a big breath.

Candy was sprawled on the ground. And it looked like someone had poured a bucket of water over her head.

CHAPTER 4

"Is she dead?" Martha's hands clenched on the handles of her walker.

"It looks like it," Pru murmured, aware of her heart banging in her chest. She'd never seen a dead body before. A trickle of blood against the brick wall caught her attention. "Maybe she banged her head and fell." She gestured to the dark stain on the brown bricks. A turned over bucket with water dribbling out of it lay on the path.

"Yeah, that could have happened – maybe." Martha sat on her walker seat. "We'd better call Mitch."

"Mitch – oh, Lauren's husband?" She was surprised she'd managed to remember that right now.

"That's him." Martha picked up her phone with a shaky hand. "Maybe you'd better do it." She held out the device.

"Okay." Pru scrolled through the list of contacts, finding a Mitch listed. She made the connection and offered the phone to Martha. "Do you want to talk to him?"

"It's Martha. Dead body, library," Martha spoke into the phone. "Yeah, I'm okay." She looked up at Pru. "He's coming. I bet he got a surprise when I told him that. He's used to Lauren and Zoe finding dead people." She shivered.

"Are you warm enough? I can see if the library has a blanket in the first aid cupboard."

"Maybe we'd better stick together. In case the killer is still around."

"Do you think this was deliberate?" Pru studied the scene.

"Unless Candy was so angry that she wasn't looking where she was going and hit the back of her head against that wall, then yes, I think someone killed her." Martha looked a little recovered. "Don't forget, I've got experience. I've helped Lauren, Annie, and Zoe with their sleuthing."

"That's right." She wasn't sure whether to believe her roommate or not. They'd only been living together for just over a week and they were still getting to know each other. And if everything Martha had told her was true, a lot of killers had roamed Gold Leaf Valley over the last few years. On the other hand, Martha had told her that it was a pretty safe town. How could it be both?

Sirens blared and two police vehicles arrived with uniformed officers. Another car pulled up in the parking lot, and a tall, dark-haired man strode toward them.

"That's Mitch," Martha told her.

Pru stared at the good-looking guy. His hair was short and dark, and his brown eyes looked serious. He wore charcoal slacks and a white button-down shirt, with a matching charcoal jacket. He greeted Martha, then turned to her.

"Martha's mentioned you to Lauren," he told her.

"All good I hope," she tried to joke.

His mouth quirked up. "Pretty much."

He took charge, taking a brief statement from each of them.

"So you didn't see anyone else in the vicinity?"

"Nope." Martha looked more like her old self. "The other members of the book club left before we did."

Mitch wrote down their names. "I'll follow up with them."

"Maybe one of them did it!" Martha looked excited.

"Why?" Pru frowned.

"I don't know yet, but I bet we can find out!"

"It's best if you leave that to me," Mitch told her firmly.

"But—"

"I don't want you to put yourself into any danger," he added.

"But you haven't been to book club like we have. See, we had to read this yucky novel about Melisande and—"

"I'll talk to the members," Mitch told her.

"Candy was very insistent that we read the book, and she got upset when none of us liked it," Pru remembered, "although we tried to be tactful about it. Well, most of us."

"That's good to know." Mitch made a note. "Martha, do you need a ride anywhere?"

"I was going to get Teddy and take him to the café. Pru was coming too because she's on her lunchbreak."

"I don't think I'll have time now." Her stomach started growling and she clapped a hand over it, hoping no one else heard it.

"I can get you a panini and bring it back to you," Martha said. "You didn't bring your lunch to work today, did you?"

"No," she replied.

"Sounds like a plan," Mitch said. "One of my officers will take you home, Martha, and then drive you and Teddy to the café. Can you make your own way back from there? Otherwise, I'm sure Lauren could drive you, and Zoe can cover for her at the café."

"I can manage to get me and Teddy home okay. We don't live far."

"Good." He smiled briefly at her.

"And then I'll bring your lunch over, Pru."

"Are you sure it won't be too much bother after all … this?" She gestured toward the uniformed officers. "I could just grab something quick from the supermarket."

"My treat," Martha said firmly.

"Thanks." Pru smiled.

Mitch allowed her to go back to work at the library. After telling her boss about Candy, she tried to focus her mind on shelving books, a task she usually enjoyed. She loved putting things into order. Her boss had looked shocked, and had rushed out to talk to the police.

Who had killed Candy? Mitch hadn't said outright it was murder, but now she had a chance to think about it, how on earth could Candy have hit her head by accident? There was no wound on her face, so it looked like she'd hit the back of her head on the brick wall. Maybe Martha was right and it was murder. But if it was an accident, where did the water come from? She would have hardly tossed the water on her own face.

By the time Pru's stomach grumbled continuously, Martha raced back into the library, a brown paper bag perched on her walker seat.

"Here," she said breathlessly, her cheeks flushed. "A turkey and cranberry panini."

"Thanks." She grabbed the bag and looked inside the generously filled sandwich. "It looks good." She glanced up at Martha. "Are you okay? You didn't rush all the way back here, did you?"

"I'm just excited about the murder." Martha's eyes lit up. "Well, you know what I mean. I'm not excited Candy is dead. But it means we can investigate."

"We can what?"

"Investigate. But this time it will be *our* murder and not Lauren, Annie, and Zoe's. Although, we might have to ask them for help if we get stuck. Huh." Her brow furrowed.

"Maybe we should talk about this outside." Pru was aware of her boss casting disapproving looks her way. Holding up her lunch bag, she gestured toward the exit. Barbara nodded.

"Good idea. We don't want anyone to overhear us." Martha trundled out of the building and around the opposite corner to where they'd found Candy.

"No." She was aware of police tape cordoning off that part of the grounds and officers going about their detecting business. "Where's Teddy?"

"At home. I dropped him off on the way back from the café. He had a good time talking to Annie while I told the girls about Candy."

Pru unwrapped the panini and took a large bite. Turkey and cranberry exploded in her mouth – delicious.

"And?" she mumbled around a mouthful, knowing she shouldn't chew and talk at the same time.

"And we should investigate – not that I told Lauren that. She doesn't like sleuthing like me, and Annie, and

Zoe do. And since we found the dead body, that means it's our case." Martha looked pleased with her reasoning.

"Don't you mean it's Mitch's case?"

"There you go, sounding like Lauren." Martha chuckled. "You two aren't twins, are you? Although you don't look alike." She eyed her figure. "Lauren's curvier than you. And her hair is light brown and shoulder-length. And yours is auburn. Her eyes are hazel and yours are green. Huh. So I don't think you're identical twins torn apart at birth. Hey, what about fraternal twins? Those are twins who are—"

"I know what fraternal twins are. Non-identical, and each twin came from a separate egg," Pru replied. "And no, I am not a twin."

"Got any other siblings?"

"Two older brothers."

"Did they boss you around growing up?"

"Sometimes."

"Maybe that's why you're a little bossy."

"*I'm* bossy?" Pru stared at her.

"Sort of. Sometimes." Martha patted her arm. "It's okay. I might be a little bossy too, at times. We'll probably even each other out."

"Because I like things to be neat and tidy?"

"Yeah." Martha nodded. "But that's probably a good thing because I can get a little sloppy at times. See? We're evening each other out already."

"Prudence?" Her boss's voice sounded from nearby. "Are you out here? Your break is almost over."

"Coming." She swallowed the last of her lunch.

"Wow, your boss is bossy, too." Martha tsked. "Poor you. Okay, I'll see you tonight and update you on our sleuthing plan."

CHAPTER 5

When Prudence arrived home that day, Teddy greeted her with a green ball in his mouth.

"I've been playing with him this afternoon, but he wants more," Martha said, sitting on the couch, her feet up on an ottoman. She looked tired.

"I'll go out to the yard with him."

"Thanks." Martha grinned.

Pru enjoyed tossing the ball for the cute puppy, who galloped to fetch it and brought it back to her, landing it at her feet. After fifteen minutes of romping in the small yard, Teddy finally started to tire.

They headed back inside, both flopping down on the sofa. Teddy snuggled in her lap and fell asleep.

"Look at that," Martha kept her voice down. "He likes you, alrighty."

"And I like him." She stroked his cotton fur, a sudden thought occurring to her. "What sort of dog is he again?"

"The shelter said he could be a Havanese mix or a Poodle/Bichon mix," Martha replied.

"What about a Coton de Tulear?"

"A what now?"

"It's a breed from Madagascar and their white coats feel like cotton. Teddy's certainly does."

"It does feel nice and soft," Martha agreed.

"They're low shedding and supposed to be low energy." Her mouth twisted wryly. "But Teddy seems to have lots of get up and go at times."

"Maybe these Coton dogs have different levels of energy. Do you mean he's a pedigree?"

"If he is a pure bred Coton, then yes."

"Ooh – wait until I tell everyone about him!"

"I don't know for sure that he is," Pru cautioned. "I guess you'd have to take him to a vet and see if they're familiar with the breed."

"That's what I'll do," Martha declared. Then she seemed to think of something. "But it might have to wait until I get my check next month. I'm still paying off my credit card bill from all the goodies I bought him."

"I understand." She was still paying off her student loans and had a long way to go.

"So let's get started with our sleuthing discussion. I'll go to the senior center tomorrow and see if I can hunt out any gossip about Candy."

"She looked a little young to be going to a place for seniors. No offense."

"I know what you mean." Martha nodded. "But you never know, someone might have known her. They might have gone to a previous book club where she forced them to read about Melisande."

"That's true," she replied slowly.

"Ruff," Teddy said sleepily, turning around in her lap.

"See? Teddy thinks it's a good idea, too." Martha beamed at her fur baby from the opposite couch. "And you can ask your boss about Candy as well – why did she want to set up the book club in the first place?"

"We know why," Pru replied. "She was fanatical about that author."

"But why?" Martha tapped her foot on the carpet. "A lot of people love certain authors but they don't go around libraries setting up book clubs and forcing people to read their books. Well, maybe a few do," she amended, "but no one I know."

"I don't know anyone like that, either."

"So why was Candy so insistent we love the book as much as she did? She got awfully upset when we told her it was yucky."

"I did say we should try to be tactful."

"Yeah, you did. Sorry if I wasn't. Sometimes I speak before I think and don't realize how it sounds until it's already out there."

"I understand." She'd barely started at the library and already had to be careful at times with the way she approached her boss, Barbara.

"So you can get some info from your boss about Candy," Martha directed. "And report back tomorrow night."

***

Martha was certainly bossy at times, Pru mused the next day as she drove to the library. On the other hand, she didn't think *she* was bossy at all – well, maybe just a tad at times. But it was certainly nicer and more efficient to live in a neat house than an untidy one.

She still shuddered at the mess her brothers' rooms had been when they were teenagers. On the few occasions when she'd gone into their bedrooms, the explosion of sloppiness certainly hadn't encouraged her to be messy herself. She could still remember the cereal bowls under their beds, covered in mold. When their mom had found out, she'd blown her top and both her brothers' rooms had become a little neater. But still.

How was she going to ask Barbara about Candy wanting to organize a book club for her favorite author, Becky Blanche? Her boss didn't encourage conversation at the best of times.

An idea suddenly hit her. A legitimate question to ask Barbara was about continuing book club now that Candy was gone. Pleased at thinking of it, she drove the rest of the way with a smile on her face.

***

"Of course we're continuing book club." Barbara stared at her, seeming aghast at the question. "I've already committed to six weeks. It's very unfortunate that Candy died, but I can't possibly cancel it now. Just carry on with it."

"Okay." Pru nodded, and hurried back to her trolley, intent on shelving the rest of the books. Just when she reached the Os, she'd realized she'd forgotten to ask anything about Candy. And judging by her boss's mood, it did not seem a good idea to go over to her and ask her about Candy again. She'd just have to tell Martha that they were not licensed detectives and to leave the solving of Candy's death to the police.

She immersed herself in her work, taking refuge in the quietness and orderliness of the library. By the time her shift was over, she was looking forward to going home to Teddy and Martha. Maybe Teddy would like to go for a walk around the block?

But when she turned into the small driveway of the yellow duplex, a car was already there. Wasn't that Mitch's vehicle? What was he doing there? Were Martha and Teddy okay?

She ran into the house. "Martha?"

"We're in here," Martha called out from the living room.

"Ruff!"

Pru's heart rate slowed down. Neither of them sounded hurt. She entered the cream and yellow room, her eyes widening at the sight of Mitch sitting on the sofa.

"I was just about to update Martha on the case."

"You were?" She frowned, sinking onto the opposite coach. Surely he didn't approve of Martha's sleuthing?

"We've discovered who Candy really was. An author by the name of Becky Blanche."

CHAPTER 6

"Huh?" Martha's mouth fell open. "Are you saying Candy was the author of that yucky book we had to read? About Melisande?"

"She was the author of *Race to the Sunset*, and some others as well," Mitch confirmed.

"So that's why she was so insistent on everyone reading that book – *her* book," Pru said slowly.

"And don't forget she asked the library to buy the copies for it," Martha added. "So she got some extra sales."

"I looked up the sales figures on the online retailers after the first book club," she remembered. "And that title wasn't selling well."

"And you didn't tell me?" Martha sounded hurt.

"Sorry. I forgot. It's been a busy week at work, getting used to my boss, and—"

"Having a new roomie." Martha nodded. "I bet that's why Candy organized this book club in the first place! To sell copies of her book. Didn't she say she was also getting a library in Sacramento to buy fifteen copies?"

"That's right." Prudence stared at her.

"I'll check out this library – do you know which branch it is?" Mitch asked.

"No," Pru replied regretfully.

"So who do you think killed her?" Martha asked eagerly.

"It's too early to tell." Mitch shook his head, his mouth quirked at the corner. "Don't worry, I'll sure I'll catch him – or her."

"Oh yeah, you're the head detective now," Martha said.

"That's right." He smiled. "Detective Castern retired, and I got promoted. But we're now looking for another detective to fill his spot."

"What about Annie?" Martha chortled.

Mitch shook his head, an amused look on his face. "You'll probably suggest Teddy as well."

"Why not?" Martha grinned. "He's such a good boy."

"I'm sure he is." Mitch smiled at the white bundle of fur sitting next to Martha on the couch, his brown button eyes curious as he listened to them talk. "It was definitely his lucky day when you adopted him from the shelter."

"And mine," Martha said in all seriousness.

Mitch refused the offer of a cup of coffee, saying he'd had one from the café earlier, and had to get going.

Pru showed him out, Martha and Teddy still sitting on the sofa.

"Look out for her," Mitch advised, "as much as you can, anyway. Sometime she gets carried away." When he saw her puzzled expression, he added, "Ask her about the gnome thief incident."

***

"Oh, that." Martha waved her hand in the air when Pru asked her what Mitch had meant about a gnome thief. "That was nothing. I was just trying to help out a friend."

"Your friend was the gnome thief?"

"No." Martha shook her head. "But it was sort of fun helping out Iris."

She noticed that Martha quickly changed the subject.

"You know, I didn't notice an author photo on the cover of that book Candy made us read – *her* book. No wonder we didn't realize she was the author."

"You're right," Pru replied slowly, thinking back. It was a shame she still didn't have a copy of *Race to the Sunset* to double check, but she was sure Martha was correct.

"That was a pretty sneaky thing to do," Martha said, her voice full of admiration.

"Perhaps she wanted to find out what everyone thought of her new novel," Pru mused.

"But she didn't like the answer," Martha pointed out. "She got real

upset that we didn't like her book."
She paused. "So, what did your boss
say about Candy?"

"She said book club will run for a
total of six weeks."

"And?" Martha asked eagerly.

"That's it."

"You didn't ask her anything else?"

"No." Pru shook her head. "Sorry."

"I guess that's because you're just
a baby sleuth, isn't that right, Teddy?"
Martha turned to her puppy, still
sitting next to her on the sofa.

"Ruff," he replied agreeably.

"And you're a …?" Pru let the
question dangle.

"An experienced sleuth. Well, sort
of. Wait until you hear what I found
out at the senior center today!"
Martha's eyes lit up.

"What?" she felt obliged to ask.

"Candy owed money to Hal's wife!"

"Pardon?"

"See, his wife Lynda sells
cosmetics on the side to supplement
their retirement. Maybe I should do
that." Martha screwed up her eyes in
thought. "Except I don't wear any

makeup. I used to sometimes when I was younger – a lot younger – but it just got to be a pain, you know?" She opened her eyes and appraised Pru. "You don't wear any – smart girl. Plus, it costs money."

"Thanks – I think." She'd wondered sometimes if she should start wearing makeup for work – subtly of course – but apart from wearing it on an occasional date, she didn't bother, either. Maybe she should try lipstick. That couldn't hurt, right?

"I know what you're thinking." Martha pointed a finger at her. "You could go and buy some from her and report back to me. It might be too obvious if I do it."

"Too obvious?" She wondered if she was in a parallel universe, the way she was parroting Martha's words.

"Yeah. She knows I'm in the same book group as her husband, and that Candy's dead – the senior center was buzzing with the news this morning – so why would I suddenly want to buy makeup from her? But she doesn't know you, so it would be perfectly okay for you to go up to her and buy a lipstick or something."

How did Martha know she'd been thinking of trying lipstick? Her eyes widened, then she blinked. It was obvious that lipstick would be one of the first cosmetics someone would buy.

"If she doesn't know me, then how would I know her, or that she's selling makeup?"

"Huh. Good point. You can tell her I told you about her – that would seem pretty natural, even if she doesn't know we're roomies yet. That will probably get out pretty soon, anyway."

"True," she agreed, although she hadn't told anyone yet. But then again, she didn't have anyone to tell in Gold Leaf Valley.

"So how do I actually buy this lipstick from her?" she asked.

"I haven't worked that out yet," Martha admitted. "But don't worry. I'll think of something."

That's what Pru was afraid of.

CHAPTER 7

Martha's new idea was to ask Hal about his wife being a suspect – at book club. Pru thought it was a terrible notion, but her roommate couldn't be swayed.

"The killer is still roaming around Gold Leaf Valley," Martha announced a week later while they ate breakfast together. "So today is a perfect day to ask Hal about his theories on the murder. And if we don't like his answers, we'll go and visit his wife, and you can buy a lipstick from her and get her talking." She sat back in her dining chair, looking pleased with her reasoning.

"Ruff!" Teddy sat next to her at the table.

"See, Teddy thinks it's a good idea, don't you, boy?" Martha beamed at him.

"Ruff!" *Yes!*

"You can't accuse Hal's wife of murder, though," Pru cautioned.

"Of course not!" Martha looked askance. "I'm not an amateur. Don't worry. I'll ask just the right sort of questions. And," she added grandly, "I've decided that we should start a club – a senior sleuthing club."

"A club?"

"Yeah. Because I'm a senior. And you and Teddy can be honorary seniors." She chuckled. "Pretty good, huh?"

"Is anyone else going to be in this club?" she asked cautiously.

"Nope. Not for now, anyway. And it's perfectly okay, because craft club only has four members and that's been going for a few years now."

"Craft club?" Her interest quickened. Maybe she needed to take up a new hobby, apart from the occasional yoga class, and she hadn't had time to find a studio in Gold Leaf Valley – if there was one.

"Yeah, it consists of Lauren, Annie, Zoe, and Mrs. Finch. And they do all sorts of crafts – well, Zoe does. Lauren knits."

"Oh."

"Have you got any hobbies?" Martha tsked at herself. "I don't think you've told me. Guess I should have asked you that before – sorry. I'm pretty busy some days, what with water color painting, my usual visits to the senior center and the café, and now I've got Teddy to look after, don't I, little guy?" She petted the puppy, who snuggled into her arm.

"Not really. I was busy studying when I was at college, but I did try to find time for yoga."

"Yoga, huh?" Martha peered across the table at her. "Can you twist yourself into a pretzel?"

"Not exactly. But I can balance on one leg. It's called Tree Pose."

"That might come in handy one day," Martha mused. "Maybe you can give me a boost to get over a wall when we're out sleuthing – you might have to stand on one leg to do it – yeah!"

Not for the first time, she wondered exactly who Martha was.

She finished eating her bran cereal, wondering if she should be more adventurous and try something different – Martha's raisin toast smelled tempting and definitely more flavorful than her bowlful of unsugared fiber, but she didn't have time today. If she didn't hurry, she would be late to work and she didn't want Barbara to frown censoriously at her.

"See you at book club." She rinsed her bowl and gathered her things.

"Can't wait!" Martha put down her half-eaten toast and grinned at her.

***

"I wasn't sure if book club was still on," Eleanor said a couple of hours later as they gathered in the cozy corner.

"I know what you mean," Ms. Tobin agreed. "It's simply dreadful that Candy was killed."

"Was she murdered?" Hal asked.

"Why do you say that?" Martha pounced on his question.

"I heard she was attacked," he replied.

"Did you hear that she was the author of the Melisande book?" Doris asked eagerly.

"No!" Eleanor said.

"I'm afraid so," Pru spoke. "Detective Denman told us last week."

"No wonder she wanted us to read her book." Ms. Tobin tsked.

Aware of her boss's frowning glance directed their way, Pru tried to bring back the members to the reason they were there – to discuss the mystery they'd read during the week.

"Did everyone finish reading *Aunt Dimity's Death*?" She held up her own copy.

"It was lovely," Ms. Tobin said.

"Yeah, it was good," Martha's tone was a little impatient. "But I think we should talk about the real murder that happened right out there." She pointed towards the exit. "Candy's death."

"Maybe you're right," Eleanor agreed. "I can't believe something like that happened – at the library!"

"Outside the library, to be precise," Hal spoke.

Martha's eyes lit up. "Did you know Candy yourself?" she asked.

"No." He frowned. "I didn't. Why would I?"

"Because your wife did!"

"What?" He reared back in his chair.

"Martha—" Pru attempted to interject, but her roommate ignored her.

"I heard that Candy owed your wife money for makeup."

"Umm ... ahh," he sputtered.

"Is that true?" Eleanor queried.

"I have no idea," he finally spoke. "That's my wife's business. She does it to make a little more money for us, but I don't know who her customers are."

"Pooh." Martha sounded disappointed.

"If we can start discussing Aunt Dimity," Pru tried again. "Doris, what did you think of it? I know you read it last week but—"

"It's still fresh in my mind," Doris replied with an eager smile. "And now I've finished book two as well. You do have book three, don't you?" she asked hopefully.

"I'm sure we do," Pru replied. If they didn't, she'd put in an order for it, or an interlibrary loan.

They began discussing the mystery, Pru pleased that book club was back on track. She glanced over at her boss at the reference desk, but Barbara was busy poring over a large, thick tome.

Toward the end of the hour, Martha said, "What book are we going to read next week?"

"Maybe we should take turns picking one," Pru suggested. "Who wants to choose?"

"I'd suggest a nice Agatha Christie, but I've read them all," Ms. Tobin said.

"And I don't read many books," Hal said.

"Why don't you choose one for us, Pru," Eleanor said, "since you work here. You should know all the good authors."

"Who do you recommend?" Doris asked. "Another mystery?"

"I wouldn't mind another one," Martha put in.

Pru racked her brains for an author she thought they'd all enjoy, finally settling on Laurie Cass, the author of the Bookmobile Cat mysteries.

"Let me check if the library has enough copies of *Checking Out Crime.*"

Luckily, there were enough paperbacks for everyone.

"Now we're all set for next week." Ms. Tobin tucked her copy into her tote bag. "I think I'll go and visit the girls at the café – would anyone like to join me?"

"Me!" Martha clambered to her feet, gripping the handles of her walker. "Hey, Doris, want to come?"

"I'd love to," Doris looked pleased at being asked, "but I have to start my shift in twenty minutes."

"At Gary's Burger Diner." Martha nodded. "Do you get free burgers?"

"During my meal break," she replied.

"That's a good perk."

"I only get one, though," Doris added. "It's not like I can make myself five burgers and eat them all, or take them home with me."

"That's quite understandable," Ms. Tobin said. "Gary needs to make enough money to pay his employees and keep everything running."

"That's true," Martha agreed.

They all said goodbye to each other, promising to read the Laurie Cass book and meet at the same time next week.

Pru breathed a sigh of relief when everyone left. It had been difficult at times to keep the members on track when they were more intrigued by Candy's murder but ... a sudden thought struck her. What if one of them was Candy's killer?

CHAPTER 8

"Tomorrow we can visit Hal's wife and ask her about Candy owing her money," Martha said that evening. They'd just finished watching an absorbing movie about a lady spy in World War II.

"Is this where I buy a lipstick?" Pru asked.

"Yep." Martha nodded. "We can say we were just passing, and I saw her house and remembered you were talking about wanting to buy some makeup, so we thought we'd stop by and see if she was home."

"That does sound pretty plausible," she admitted.

"I thought so, too." Martha beamed.

"Ruff!" Teddy agreed, looking relaxed and happy on the sofa next to Martha.

"What time do you finish work tomorrow? We don't want to walk around in the dark – that might look suspicious."

"I finish at three."

"Goody. We can hit the streets as soon you get home. Ooh – you can walk Teddy – if you don't mind," Martha added. "I don't want to get his lead tangled up in my walker wheels."

"It will be a pleasure." Pru smiled at the puppy.

"Ruff!" *Goody!*

***

As soon as Pru arrived home the next day, Martha pounced on her. "Let's go!"

"Already?"

"The sooner we visit, the sooner we might get some answers," Martha said briskly. "I'm all set – see?"

Pru did see – Martha's wore her turquoise sweatpants outfit, and Teddy wore a matching collar – and leash.

"Teddy's all set, too." Martha handed the lead to her.

"So I see." She couldn't help smiling down at the little white puppy. "Okay."

They walked along the street, Pru taking the time to look at the other Victorian era houses.

"I forgot to tell you that Gold Leaf Valley is a Gold Rush town," Martha said, pushing her walker. "That's why there are so many cute Victorians, but mine is a fake."

"I did wonder," Pru replied tactfully.

"But I love it." Martha grinned.

"Ruff!" Teddy walked sedately on the lead, only stopping occasionally to sniff at an interesting blade of grass. It was as if he knew they were on a sleuthing mission.

"Is Hal's wife going to be home?" she asked.

"I hope so," Martha replied. "She wasn't at the senior center today, so if she's not out selling makeup, she should be there."

"How are you going to ask about Candy's murder without being too obvious?"

"Leave it to me, roomie." Martha winked. "Watch and learn."

They turned a corner and walked down another street, some of the houses definitely showing their age.

"Some of these cottages need a new coat of paint," Martha observed. "Ooh – here we are."

They stopped outside a small, blue Victorian that was better kept than some of its neighbors on the street. "This is where Hal and his wife Lynda live."

Martha trundled along the little concrete path that led to the front door.

Pru followed, Teddy tugging slightly at the lead to encourage her to walk a little faster.

Martha pressed the doorbell.

Ding dong.

The door opened.

"Hello?" A woman with salt and pepper hair cut in a neat, short style, peered at them, her expression clearing when she said, "Oh, it's you, Martha. What can I do for you?"

"Pru here was just talking about needing to buy some makeup when I realized we were in your street," Martha replied blithely. "So of course I told her she had to buy some from you."

"That's very kind of you." Lynda smiled, her lips painted in a becoming rose shade. "Come in. Oh – is that little Teddy?" She bent down stiffly to greet him. "You've mentioned him at the senior center."

"Ruff," Teddy said quietly, sniffing her outstretched palm.

"Isn't he a good boy?" Lynda straightened up. "Let's see what I've got for you, dear."

Pru followed Martha and Teddy inside the house, impressed despite herself by Martha's fibbing.

They ended up in the beige carpeted living room, the furniture consisting of a pale blue lounge suite and a mahogany coffee table.

"Now, what were you thinking of?" Lynda eyed Pru critically. "You don't really need to wear any makeup, although I shouldn't be talking myself out of a sale. I thought men liked the fresh-faced look these days."

"Probably," Martha replied, "but Pru here was thinking of a new lipstick – in case she goes on a date."

"Oh, do you have someone in mind?" Lynda looked interested.

"No." Pru's eyes widened. "I'm new in town and I've been busy at work. I haven't had time to meet anyone, let alone—"

"That's why she needs a new lipstick," Martha cut in, "so she can meet a hottie and then go on a date with him."

"Of course." Lynda nodded, as if that made perfect sense to her. "Well, let's see what I've got. I'll get my supplies." She hurried out of the room.

"Martha, do you really think this is a good idea?" Pru murmured. "What if—"

Lynda came back in. "Did you say something, dear?"

"She was just wondering what color she should try. Wasn't she, Teddy?"

Martha winked at the puppy, sitting on the carpet next to her walker.

"Ruff!" His brown eyes sparkled.

"What about pink?" Lynda looked at Pru critically. "Not too bright."

"That sounds nice," she replied, relieved.

"She'll never get a guy with a boring color like that," Martha broke in. "What about a hot red?"

"Let's see." Lynda rummaged around in her large kit. "What about this one?" She revealed a fierce red shade.

"Yeah!"

"No!" Pru blinked at the traffic stopping color.

"For some reason, this is not a good seller." Lynda put it back in her case with a frown. "Maybe something a little less red." She showed Pru a nice pink.

"Well, I suppose," Martha said doubtfully.

"Let's put some on your hand," Lynda suggested, "and then you can hold it against your face. Here's a mirror." She handed Pru an oval mirror with a handle.

She applied the lipstick to the back of her hand and held it near her lips. The shade wasn't as bad as she thought, and in fact it might even flatter her a little.

"That looks good," Martha said in approval. "She'll take it."

"I will?" Pru raised an eyebrow at her roommate.

"If you like it," Martha added hastily.

"It is nice," she said tactfully.

"Wonderful!" Lynda sounded pleased. "Now, is there anything else you'd like to look at? Eyeshadow, blush, concealer—"

"Not today," Martha broke in. "Pru was just thinking about a lipstick. You've been selling this stuff for a while, haven't you?"

"Yes," Lynda replied. "It gives me a little extra income."

"That's what your husband said at book club." Martha nodded. "But what do you do if people don't pay you after they get the makeup?"

Lynda pursed her lips. "That rarely happens."

"Huh. Because I heard that Candy owed you money."

Lynda paled. "How did you know that?"

"People." Martha waved a hand in the air. "But how did she come to owe you money for makeup?"

Lynda frowned. "She'd bought it from me a couple of times before, so when she said she was a little short that week but needed to look good for a meeting, what could I say? Obviously now, I should have said no money, no cosmetics, but—" she sighed "—I felt sorry for her." Her voice hardened. "That was my mistake. Because now I'm out forty-nine dollars and she got to wear the makeup. And now we find out she was an author! She was probably making more money than me!"

"If it makes you feel any better, I don't think her books were selling very well," Pru said. "I looked up her online sales figures."

"You can do that?" Lynda looked interested.

"Anyone can on the online retailers – the ones that display them," she replied.

"That's why we think she started this book club – so the library would buy her books," Martha commented.

"Ruff!"

"What a sweet boy you are." Lynda glanced down at Teddy. "Look at how good he's being, Martha. I don't know why they won't let you bring him to the senior center."

"Me neither." Martha's mouth tilted downwards. "But anyway, since me and Pru found Candy's body, we need to check where everyone was at the time of her murder."

"Martha." Pru drew in a breath. Wasn't that being *too* obvious?

"I know where you're going with this and of course I didn't kill her," Lynda replied. "Really, Martha, how could you think such a thing?"

"Of course I don't think that *now*," Martha said, "but if you don't tell us where you were at the time, then we'll probably start thinking that eventually – if we don't catch the killer beforehand."

"That makes sense – I suppose," Lynda said reluctantly. "If you must know, I was out selling makeup door to door to my regular customers. And I took some orders, so they'll be able to verify my whereabouts – or should that be my alibi?"

"That's good." Martha nodded in approval. "Thanks."

"But I'm not the one you should be talking to. Did you know that Candy made Doris remake her burger five times at Gary's Diner? If that doesn't give someone a motive to kill her, what does?"

CHAPTER 9

"Huh?" Martha's mouth fell open.

"Haven't you heard that piece of gossip?" Lynda asked in satisfaction. She tsked. "Maybe you're slipping, Martha."

"Never!" Martha recovered. "When was this?"

"Yes, when?" Pru added. She'd only just met Doris, but she liked her. How on earth could she have killed Candy?

"Recently. Apparently Doris was in tears and Gary eventually had to take over and cook the burger just right."

"That doesn't make sense." Martha frowned. "Doris has been working there a while and the burgers are always good. Especially the smoky barbecue special."

"Be that as it may," Lynda said, "that's what I heard. And I got it from Cindy, the waitress there. She couldn't believe that Candy was being so picky about it all."

"But why would Doris kill Candy over something like that?" Pru frowned.

"I don't know, dear," Lynda said. "That's for the police to find out." She glanced at her friend. "Exactly why are you looking into this, Martha? I don't see you wearing a badge deputizing you."

"That's because Mitch – Detective Denman – hasn't gotten around to it." Martha chuckled. "You know I love a mystery – and I've helped the girls at the café in the past with their sleuthing."

"That's true," Lynda conceded. "Well, if Candy upset two people in Gold Leaf Valley – myself and Doris – who else had she upset before she died? She didn't visit the senior center, so I don't know how you're going to find out anything else about her."

***

"Our next move will be checking the burger story with Doris," Martha announced on the walk home.

Teddy walked briskly on the lead, only stopping once or twice to sniff enticing blades of grass, and the occasional fence post.

"When are we going to do that?" Pru asked.

"Feel like a burger tonight?" Martha's eyes lit up.

Which is how Pru found herself sitting at a table inside Gary's Burger Diner a short while later. They'd taken Teddy home and made him comfy with his own meal, and special soft rabbit, telling him to be a good boy while they were out.

The eatery was all stainless steel and glass, but had a pleasant vibe. Several customers were enjoying their food, while a few more sat at tables with hungry expressions, and there was a low buzz of conversation.

"Hey, Cindy." Martha snagged the waitress's attention. The twenty-something girl wore her long blonde hair swept back with violet barrettes. "Is Doris working now?"

"Yes, she is. Did you want to talk to her for a sec?"

"Could we?"

"Maybe it's not a good time," Pru warned, wondering not for the first time if this "sleuthing" was a good idea. "Doris might be busy filling orders."

"I'm sure she could take a break for a few minutes," Cindy replied. "She's been telling me about book club at the library and how you encouraged her to try a different book. You're Pru, right?" She smiled. "Now she reads her novel on her breaks here."

"That's great." Pru smiled back.

"Would you like to order now and then chat to Doris?"

"Yes." Martha pointed to the menu. "I'll have the smoky barbecue special and a chocolate shake."

"I guess I'll have the same," Pru said, keen to find out if the burger was as good as Martha seemed to think.

"I'll see if Doris can talk to you for a minute." Cindy wrote down the order and dashed to the kitchen. A few seconds later, she returned. "Doris said she can chat to you while she's working – she has a pile of orders to get through. Gary won't be back for about twenty minutes, so I can sneak you in."

"Let's go!" Martha grabbed the handles of her walker and made a beeline toward the kitchen.

"How are you finding Gold Leaf Valley?" Cindy asked Pru.

"I haven't been here long, but I like it so far. Everyone seems to know everyone else, though."

"That's one of the benefits of small-town life," Cindy replied. "But it does have its drawbacks at times, too. Everyone seems to know what everyone else is doing."

"Apart from the police knowing who killed Candy."

"That's true," Cindy conceded. "But they'll probably catch him before long."

"You don't think it could be a woman?"

Cindy stopped and stared at her. "You know, you're right. I hadn't really thought of that. Gosh, I think a female killer is scarier somehow than a male!"

Martha pushed open the swinging kitchen door. "Yoo hoo, Doris."

"Hi." Doris looked flushed as she flipped two burgers on the grill. "I'm sorry I can't take a proper break to talk to you, but the customers keep giving me orders to fill."

"I'm sorry we're bothering you at work," Pru said.

"It's no bother." Doris flashed a smile at her. "I can talk and cook at the same time – as long as Gary isn't here."

"Yeah, he's a stickler for health and safety," Cindy put in. "I'd better get back to the dining room."

"What can I do for you?" Doris asked, flicking a glance toward the other kitchen hand, who was plating the orders. The savory aroma of barbecue sauce and fried hamburger filled the kitchen, making Pru's mouth water.

The grill hissed as Doris slapped on another three patties.

"We heard that Candy made you recook her burger five times," Martha said.

"Who told you that?" Doris swung around, a spatula in her hand.

"Someone who was here when it happened."

Doris drew in a breath. "It's true. It had just been one of those days, you know? Where nothing goes right. And this order – Candy's, I later discovered – was a real pain. It's a burger – not a piece of filet mignon. First she wanted it medium to well done. Then she wanted it more medium. Then she practically wanted it raw because she said I'd burned it when I hadn't. Then she wanted it medium again." Bright spots of color dotted Doris's cheeks. "I got more and more aggravated until Gary eventually took over. I don't know what he did, but she didn't complain anymore."

"Did you get in trouble?" Pru asked.

"No." Doris shook her head. "Gary was very understanding and said that sort of thing has happened to him, too. I just don't know why Candy made such a big deal about it all. The burger Gary cooked for her looked exactly the same as the first one I'd made for her."

"Wow," Pru murmured.

"That's not nice." Martha frowned. "No wonder someone killed Candy if she acted like that all the time."

"You think I killed her?" Doris pointed the spatula at her grease-splattered chest.

"No," Pru told her.

"Not really," Martha replied. "But someone did, and me and Pru – and Teddy – are investigating."

"Where is he?" Doris looked around the kitchen, as if expecting to spot the puppy any second.

"I left him at home because he's not allowed in Gary's." Martha pouted.

"That's a shame. He's such a cute little thing."

"Isn't he?" Martha beamed.

"So what happened after Candy was satisfied with the burger Gary cooked for her?" Pru tried to get them back on track.

Doris shrugged. "I heard from Cindy that Gary actually gave it to her on the house."

"Huh." Martha frowned. "That sounds like a good way of getting a free meal – complain enough that they'll do anything to keep you happy."

"I hadn't thought of that." Doris's eyebrows rose. "No wonder she was never satisfied with the way I cooked it."

"What if Candy was short of money?" Pru pondered.

"Yeah!" Martha pointed a finger at her, then turned to Doris. "Thanks. I can't wait for my burger – I know you'll make it super yummy." She grinned.

CHAPTER 10

"This is making sense," Martha announced a short time later, after she'd polished off her smoky barbecue burger, plus onion rings and fries – as well as slurping up a chocolate shake.

Pru marveled at her appetite. She'd even given her roommate a few of her fries and onion rings.

"You mean Candy didn't have much money?"

"Exactly." Martha nodded. "If her books weren't selling, and she didn't pay for her cosmetics, and now she scored a free burger – probably with all the trimmings – what else did she get up to, to get stuff for free?"

"All I can think of is how she organized book clubs at the libraries in the area so they would have to buy her book and she'd earn royalties," Pru admitted. "Remember, she mentioned a library in Sacramento who bought fifteen copies of *Race to the Sunset*."

"That's right." Martha's eyes lit up. "I guess we should investigate that next."

"Wouldn't Mitch – Detective Denman – do that?"

"Probably. But what if he doesn't ask the same questions we would?"

"He does know you're poking around in this, doesn't he?" She finished her shake, unable to help the discreet slurp at the end.

"He knows I like sleuthing."

Which wasn't an exact answer.

"Would you like anything else?" Cindy appeared.

"Not for me." Pru patted her stomach. She hoped she hadn't eaten too much – but Martha was right – the food had been delicious.

"Nor me." Martha sounded regretful. "It was super yummy, though. Be sure to tell Doris for me, won't you?"

"I will." Cindy smiled. "Hey," she leaned towards them, "you know how you were talking about book club before? Well, there was another customer in here that day when Candy was here complaining about her meal, who's also in your group."

"Really?" Pru asked.

"How do you know?"

"Doris told me. She looked to be in her late forties and had this kind of elegance about her. And she wore this really smart suit and carried this really classy old school purse. I don't know her name, though."

"That sounds like Eleanor." Martha sounded excited.

"It does," Pru said thoughtfully.

"Did she nit-pick about her burger?" Martha asked.

"No." Cindy shook her head. "But she did look over at Candy a few times when she was complaining. A lot of customers did, though. Candy made sure everyone knew she was dissatisfied."

"Maybe that's why she was a little snarky with Candy at book club," Pru remembered back to the first meeting.

"Yeah, I wondered what her problem was with Candy, but I didn't like to say," Martha replied.

"Well, I've got to take some more orders, so I'll see you guys around." Cindy smiled at them. "I'm glad you enjoyed your meal."

"You betcha!"

***

"Now we have to talk to Eleanor," Martha said later that evening when they were relaxing in the living room.

"And ask her what?" Pru's tone was skeptical.

"If she noticed anything funny about Candy when she was at Gary's Burger Diner."

"Apart from complaining about her meal five times so she could get a free one?"

"Exactly!"

"But what would she say?"

"She could explain to us why she was there in the first place," Martha said after a few seconds. "She acts like a posh lady, so why is she slumming it at Gary's? Not that Gary's isn't a good place to eat," she added quickly. "And it's nice and clean and has good food."

"I understand your point," Pru replied reluctantly. "Maybe she's short of money too, so instead of eating at a fancy restaurant, she decided to get more for her money at Gary's?"

"Ooh – good one." Martha patted Teddy, who sat next to her as usual on the sofa. "Isn't it, little guy?"

"Ruff!" Teddy nodded his white furry head, his brown eyes gleaming with interest.

"But I don't see how we're going to bump into her," Pru said.

"Don't you have her contact details?" Martha eyed her.

"No."

"What about the book club sign up information?"

"Most people just put their first names and an email or phone number," Pru explained. "And you didn't write yours down because I asked you to come."

"Huh." Martha thought for a moment. "What about her library card details? I bet you can find out what they are."

"No, I cannot," Pru said firmly. "Firstly, it would be a breach of privacy, and secondly, I don't know what her surname is, so I couldn't even if I wanted to. Which I don't."

"Oh, all right." Martha heaved a sigh. "But it was a good idea, wasn't it, Teddy?"

"Ruff!"

"I guess we could ask her if she noticed something when she's at book club next week," Pru said. "Unless you know her, like Lynda."

"I haven't seen her at the senior center," Martha admitted, "or at Annie's café. Ooh – I could ask Lauren and Zoe if they know her!"

"That does sound like a good idea," she conceded.

"You could come with me!" Martha sounded excited. "It's time you met everyone, anyway. What time do you get off work tomorrow?"

"Four."

"Perfect! If you rush home, we should just have time to get there before they close at five."

CHAPTER 11

The next day, Pru found it hard to concentrate on her work. She'd almost shelved a whole trolley of books incorrectly, and typed the wrong name on a man's library card, so consumed with thinking about the upcoming visit to the café. Martha had talked so much about it – would she be disappointed if it didn't live up to her roommate's enthusiastic descriptions?

When she arrived home, Martha and Teddy were waiting.

"Goody – you're here."

"Ruff!" Teddy looked cute in his matching blue collar and lead, complementing Martha's blue sweatpants and sweater. "If we take your car, we can get there faster."

"Okay." Pru ushered them into her small, silver SUV, and followed Martha's directions to the Norwegian Forest Cat Café.

The Victorian era building was painted pale yellow on the outside, with large plate glass windows showing the pine tables and chairs available to customers.

"I'm gonna get me a hot chocolate – with plenty of marshmallows." Martha winked. "What do you want? My treat."

"That's kind of you," Pru replied. It had been a busy day. "Maybe a latte?"

"Lauren makes the best ones."

Pru fetched the walker out of the trunk, and held Teddy's lead as she opened the oak and glass entrance door.

The interior walls were the same pale yellow and the atmosphere was warm and welcoming. A string-art picture of a cupcake with lots of pink frosting decorated one of the walls, and the old wooden floorboards creaked when Pru entered.

"Brrt!" A large, silver-gray tabby with long fur and a plumy tail scampered over to them, and jumped onto the walker seat.

"Ruff!" Teddy greeted his pal.

"Brrt," the tabby replied, looking down at him, and patted the space on the seat next to her.

"That's Annie," Martha informed her. "Teddy usually shares the walker with her."

"Oh." Pru picked up the puppy and deposited him gently on the seat. "There you go."

"Ruff!" Teddy's eyes sparkled, before turning his attention to Annie. They touched noses, and settled onto the seat together.

"Hi, Martha!" A slim brunette with a pixie cut zipped over to them. "What can we get you?" She eyed Pru with interest. "Have we met? I'm Zoe, and this is Lauren." She pointed to the curvy girl with shoulder-length light brown hair with hints of gold behind the counter. Lauren waved.

"This is who I've been telling you about," Martha said. "My roomie, Pru."

"Oh, you're the assistant librarian," Lauren said.

"Yes." Pru nodded.

"Welcome to Gold Leaf Valley."
Lauren smiled.

"Thanks."

"Brrt!" *Welcome!*

Pru picked up Teddy when Martha started pushing the walker, following the silver-tabby's brrts and brrps to a large table near the counter. She followed with Teddy. When Martha parked the walker, she gently placed the puppy on the black vinyl padded seat so he could sit next to his friend again.

"Annie seats everyone," Zoe told her.

"Really?" Although, they were the only customers at the moment.

"You'll have to come back when it's busier and see for yourself," Lauren told her.

"Good idea." Martha nodded. "Now, I'll have my usual hot chocolate and Pru said she wanted a latte."

"Coming right up." Lauren began grinding the beans. Notes of hazelnut and spices wafted through the air.

"We've sold out of cupcakes," Zoe said mournfully, "otherwise we'd give you one on the house."

"What sort were they?" Pru asked, eyeing the empty glass case where only a few crumbs remained.

"Triple chocolate ganache, lavender, and blueberry crumble today," Lauren answered, steaming the milk. She flicked a glance at Zoe.

"Oops!" Zoe zipped behind the counter and fetched a container of mini pink and white marshmallows.

"I'll have to come back another time and buy one," Pru said, tempted by the descriptions. She settled at the table with Martha and the fur babies. Her eyes widened a tad as Annie hopped off the walker seat and onto one of the pine chairs close to it, Teddy following her example, until they each sat on their own seat around the table.

"That's how you do it, cutie pie." Martha winked at Annie.

"Brrt!"

Lauren brought the beverages over, placing the latte in front of Pru.

"Wow." She stared at the skillfully created peacock on top of the micro foam.

"We did an advanced latte art course a while ago." Zoe smiled. "But Lauren's better at it than I am."

"You're pretty good, too," Lauren replied.

"It looks wonderful," Pru said.

"Lots of marshmallows – goody." Martha dipped her spoon into her cocoa, and came up with a brown, pink, and white frothy concoction. "Never buy your coffee or cupcakes anywhere else," she advised Pru. "Or hot chocolate, of course."

"Not that there is anywhere around here, really," Zoe mused. "This café used to belong to Lauren's Gramms, and when she inherited it, she turned it into a certified cat café. And then I came to visit her one weekend and stayed because I loved it so much." She giggled. "We're cousins, in case Martha hasn't told you that."

"Oh." That seemed to explain a bit. She dipped her spoon into the foam, sorry to break up the pretty design, but she needed caffeine.

The coffee was a good strength, and the milk had been textured expertly. Martha was right – this really was the best place to grab a latte.

"You're not usually here so late, Martha," Zoe observed, plonking down on one of the empty chairs.

"Pru didn't get off work til four," Martha mumbled around another spoonful of gooey half-melted marshmallows, "and we wanted to ask you if you know this posh lady called Eleanor."

"Eleanor?" Lauren joined them at the table and looked quizzically at Zoe.

"Nope," Zoe replied.

"She's a member of our book club," Pru explained.

"Yeah, and you'll never guess what happened!" Martha leaned forward, excitement flickering across her face. "One of our members was murdered!"

"We know." Lauren nodded. "You told us the other day and—"

"Oh, yeah – I forgot for a second that I already told you, and that Mitch would tell you about his murders as well." Martha pouted.

"But Zoe and I didn't know Candy," Lauren said.

"She didn't come in here and complain about her coffee or cupcake?" Pru asked. Although why anyone would have the nerve to, she had no idea.

"Nope," Zoe replied.

"She did that at Gary's," Martha put in. "She made poor Doris the kitchen hand cook her burger five times and still complained – but she ended up getting her whole meal for free!"

"No way!" Zoe's mouth parted.

"But I thought you wanted to know about Eleanor," Lauren said.

"Oh, yeah." Martha nodded. "Because I haven't seen her at the senior center, so I thought she might be one of your customers."

"What does she look like?" Lauren asked. "Maybe she just comes for a to-go order and we don't know her name."

"She's posh, and wears smart suits and has an old handbag that looks like it was very expensive years ago and still looks good," Martha said.

"I can't remember seeing a woman like that in here," Zoe finally said.

"Me neither," Lauren added.

"Brrt!" Annie agreed.

"It must be true if Annie says so." Martha winked at the silver-gray tabby.

"Ruff!"

They all chuckled.

"I'm sorry we can't help you, Martha." Zoe sounded disappointed. "You know how we like sleuthing."

"You mean you and Annie do," Lauren pointed out.

"Brrt!"

"Since Pru and I found Candy's body, I'm thinking of this as *my* murder case." Martha looked at Lauren, Zoe, and Annie a little apologetically. "I hope you understand."

"Of course we do," Zoe replied. "I'd think exactly the same way."

"I knew you'd be okay with it." Martha nodded happily. "And I've even started a senior sleuthing club!"

"Really?" Lauren crinkled her brow. "Who's in it?"

"Just me and Teddy – and Pru," Martha replied. "But since I'm the senior and head sleuth, I thought I could call it that."

"Good one." Zoe grinned.

"You will be careful, won't you, Martha?" Lauren fretted.

"You betcha." Martha nodded. "Well, as careful as I can be." She winked.

"I'll be around," Pru tried to reassure them.

"Thanks." Lauren smiled.

"I hope you'll be able to keep up with Martha." Zoe giggled.

"Brrt!"

CHAPTER 12

"Well, that was a nice visit, but disappointing that the girls didn't know anything about Eleanor or Candy," Martha said when they left the café and got back to the car.

"What's our next move?" Pru surprised herself by asking.

Martha grinned. "I've got you hooked, haven't I? Watch out – sleuthing is addictive!"

Pru shook her head as she put Martha's walker in the trunk. Her roommate constantly surprised her.

They drove home and Martha heated up a can of chili.

"Lemme know when you want to do some cooking," Martha said.

"Should we write up a schedule?" she asked.

"Ruff!" Teddy walked around the kitchen, his nose to the floor.

"You'd better not have any of this stuff," Martha warned him. "I shouldn't be having any either according to my doctor – but pooh – what does he know?"

"Does Teddy need feeding?" Pru asked.

"I was just about to do that." Martha nodded to the can on the counter. "Just got it out of the fridge."

Pru ladled the beefy chunks into Teddy's bowl, and he started chowing down.

"So what do you think about making a cooking schedule?" Pru tried again.

"I guess that's a good idea." Martha nodded. "I hope you like the same food I do, though."

"I have so far," Pru said cautiously. "How hot is this chili, though?"

"Don't worry, it's mild." Martha gave it another stir. "Okay, so put down one night for pizza, and one night for burgers."

"That's five nights left."

"Two nights each – and I'll cook the third night," Martha said generously.

"Are you sure?" Pru looked at her. "I don't mind."

"But you've worked all day," Martha said. "I hope you know some good recipes. I like using a can now and then but I also like real food."

"I know what you mean," she replied. "I can make chicken pot pie – with frozen pastry."

"Good." Martha nodded encouragingly. "What else?"

"Pancakes?" She'd realized she'd started missing the motel's pancake breakfast.

"Ooh – we could have pancakes for dinner one night – with bacon!"

"Ruff!" Teddy had finished his dinner and looked up at the sound of the word bacon.

"I don't think bacon is good for dogs," Pru said apologetically to him.

"Pooh!" Martha pouted.

They discussed other dinner ideas until the chili was ready to serve.

"We have to find out if Eleanor noticed anything else funny about Candy at Gary's Burger Diner, and why she was there in the first place." Martha scraped her chili bowl clean.

Pru admitted to herself that the canned meal had been delicious and if it was her turn to cook one night and she had no ideas, she'd resort to heating one up for them.

"How are we going to do that? Apart from asking her at the next book club?"

"We might have to wait until then," Martha grumbled, "since nobody seems to know who Eleanor is. Pooh."

***

Unfortunately, Martha was right. Pru immersed herself in a book on the weekend, and was busy at the library the following week. Martha was fresh out of ideas, but she'd perked up on the morning of the next book club.

"Okay, this is what we're gonna do," Martha announced at breakfast, munching on her raisin toast. "We're gonna ask Eleanor today about noticing anything strange about Candy that day at Gary's, and if she wants to know why we're asking, we'll tell her she could have important info for the case she doesn't realize she has." Martha looked pleased at her reasoning.

"When do you think Lauren's husband will find the killer?" Pru asked.

"He's taking his time," Martha tsked. "I called Lauren on the weekend for an update, but she didn't have one. And then I called Zoe, in case she knew something extra but she didn't." Martha pouted. "So it's up to us to solve the case."

"Ruff!" Teddy sat on the chair next to Martha, his ears pricked and his brown eyes shining.

"You'll have to stay home today, little guy." Martha petted him. "Since some people don't like you being in the library." She gave Pru a pointed look.

"It's not that I don't like him in the library," she attempted to explain, "it's that he's not allowed. If you want him to accompany you everywhere, then you need to look into him becoming a certified service dog."

"I think I'll do that." Martha nodded. "Right after we catch this killer!"

***

The remaining members arrived on time for book club – apart from Hal.

"Hal made this group sound so interesting, I had to come and visit myself." Lynda's salt and pepper hair was styled neatly, and she wore olive slacks and a plum sweater. "I hope that's okay, Pru."

"Of course." She nodded. "But Hal could have come as well."

"Between you and me, I don't think this is quite his thing. I admit, I pushed him into coming because I thought it would do him good, but when his brother invited him to take a drive to Zeke's Ridge today, I told him it was okay."

"We should go there one day," Martha said, sitting comfortably in one of the armchairs. "Teddy would love it!"

"Oh, yes, you must visit it," Ms. Tobin added. "It's a charming little place, although it's even smaller than Gold Leaf Valley."

The group chuckled.

"Well, let's get started." Pru picked up her copy of *Checking Out Crime.*

"Another good mystery," Ms. Tobin said happily. "I don't know how these writers come up with all their plots. Just look at Agatha Christie – she wrote so many books! – yet the plots are always satisfying."

"That reminds me." Martha tapped the cover of her book. "Eleanor, what were you doing at Gary's?"

"Excuse me?" Eleanor started, blinking in surprise.

"You know – that day when Candy wasn't satisfied about her burger."

"Oh – that." Eleanor's expression cleared. "I'd heard how delicious the burgers were there, so I decided to try one for myself."

"What did you think?" Ms. Tobin asked.

"I couldn't fault it," Eleanor admitted.

"So why did Candy make such a fuss about sending her burger back so many times?" Martha patted Doris's hand. "Did you notice anything strange?"

"Like what?" Eleanor asked.

"Like … like … Candy doing something funny to her burger to make it taste bad!"

Doris turned to look at Martha, her mouth parting.

"Why would she do something like that?" Eleanor demanded. "Even though I detested that book she made us read, why would she get up to something like that?"

"To score a free meal," Doris replied. "Which is what ended up happening. Although, she just complained the patty wasn't cooked right."

"Doris, your burgers are a pleasure to eat." Lynda shook her head. "It makes no sense that Candy would behave that way. I thought she was a successful author, although …" She fell silent and Pru wondered if she was thinking of the cosmetics money Candy had owed her.

"Perhaps we should discuss the book," she suggested, aware of her boss's sharp glance. This morning, Barbara was checking out a pile of books, scanning each barcode.

Lynda squinted at Eleanor. "Did you go to a writer's group years ago?" she finally asked. "At someone's house? It would be around ten years ago."

"I did dabble," Eleanor replied. "But I realized it wasn't for me." She frowned across the circle at Lynda. "You do look vaguely familiar."

"Ten years is a long time when you're our age," Lynda chuckled. "That must be why I feel I've seen you somewhere before. I only went to one meeting."

"Where do you hang out, Eleanor?" Martha inquired. "I asked around at the senior center, but nobody had heard of you. And the girls at the café said you're not one of their customers, either."

"I don't consider myself old enough to be a senior," Eleanor replied frostily. "Really, Martha. And as for visiting a café, I prefer making my own coffee at home with a French press. It's far superior to anything I could buy anywhere."

"I don't know," Pru felt obliged to put in. "I had a latte at the café last week and it was excellent. And I got a peacock design on it."

"The girls are very good at their latte art, aren't they?" Ms. Tobin said. "I do enjoy my visits there. In fact, I'm going to visit them when we finish up here. Would anyone like to join me?"

"Me," Martha said eagerly. "But I've got to get Teddy first."

"I'll come," Lynda said. "Of course, I've been there before, but unfortunately I have to watch my pennies these days. Otherwise I'd probably be a daily customer."

The group chuckled.

Pru realized that Eleanor hadn't answered Martha's question about where she "hung out".

"Are you a local, Eleanor?" she asked politely.

"No. I live in one of those new subdivisions on the way to Sacramento," Eleanor replied.

"Fancy." Martha grinned.

"It's not exactly what I'm used to," Eleanor admitted, "but it will do – for now."

No one seemed to know what to say to that, so Pru asked a question about the book, and managed to get the group back on track.

When the clock finally nudged eleven o'clock, her boss approached. "Pru, I need you to get the room set up for French conversation."

"Of course, Barbara. We just need to choose a book for next week's discussion."

"Very well." Barbara strode back to the desk.

"She's not real friendly, is she?" Martha observed.

"Barbara has run the library for years," Ms. Tobin said. "I heard she was very upset when Pru's predecessor left."

"Why was that?" she asked. There hadn't been much talk in the break

148

room about the woman she'd replaced.

"She ran off to get married and I'm afraid Barbara didn't take the news very well."

"That's what I heard, too," Lynda said.

"I hope she's happy," Pru remarked.

"Cindy at the diner told me she'd sent a postcard to a friend – all the way from Switzerland!" Doris sounded impressed. "They're going to travel the world!"

"Wow." Pru was impressed.

"No wonder old bossy boots walks around like she has a pooey smell under her nose," Martha said. "I bet she's jealous."

"Which book are we going to read for next week?" she tried to get everyone's attention. "Who would like to choose?"

They eventually decided on a reliable Agatha Christie, Ms. Tobin recommending the first Poirot, *The Mysterious Affair at Styles.*

"I'm sure you'll enjoy it, Doris," she reassured her. "Have you seen the Poirot television series? Simply marvelous!"

"No," Doris replied. "I'll see if I can watch it online."

"That Poirot's good." Martha nodded. "I bet Teddy would like to watch him and pick up some tips."

Pru had to stop herself from giggling, and she couldn't help wondering if Martha would suggest that she watch the TV show too, to pick up some hints as well.

She checked out everyone's book for them, noticing Doris was already flicking through her copy. Waving goodbye to everyone, she was about to set up the room for French conversation when Martha stopped her.

"Senior sleuthing club meeting tonight after dinner!"

CHAPTER 13

"I've just had the best idea," Martha told her that evening, after they'd finished their meal of corned beef hash. It had been Martha's turn to cook, and Pru had thoroughly enjoyed it.

"What is it?"

"We need to check on Lynda's cosmetic customers to see if she was telling the truth about visiting them when Candy was murdered," Martha informed her.

"That *is* a good idea," Pru admitted.

"Ruff!" *Yes!*

"But how do we find out who they are?"

"Hmm." Martha scrunched up her face. "Good question. Remember when we visited her and she said her customers would verify her alibi? So all we have to do is ask her who they are. If she acts shady, then obviously she's hiding something."

"Does she go to the senior center?"

"Sometimes. I know what you're thinking." Martha grinned and pointed a finger at her. "I should go there tomorrow and if Lynda's there, just ask her."

Pru nodded.

"And you and me – and Teddy—" Martha looked fondly at the puppy "— can do some more investigating."

"Ruff!" Teddy tilted his head in a nod.

"See?" Martha stroked his soft white fur. "Teddy loves sleuthing – just like me."

***

When Pru arrived home from work the next day, she wondered if Martha had made any progress on the case. Then she brought herself up short – now she was starting to think like an amateur sleuth! What happened to the Pru who had been content – no, make that thrilled – to have her first job as assistant librarian – the first rung on the ladder to a library career?

It was all she had ever wanted – or so she'd thought.

Now, she was a participant in Martha's sleuthing schemes – and she wasn't complaining. Not yet, anyway.

"Oh, goody, you're home." Martha beamed at her when she walked into the living room. Turning off the TV with the remote, she said, "We were watching one of those game shows where you can win lots of money if you get the questions right – but Teddy and I thought the questions were a bit boring, didn't we?"

"Ruff!" Teddy sat next to Martha on the sofa.

"It's a shame they weren't about Agatha Christie," Pru joked. "Ms. Tobin would probably be able to answer them all."

"Good one." Martha chuckled. "Or about hot chocolate – I bet I could get all those right."

"Did you find out anything at the senior center today?"

"You betcha! I've got a list of Lynda's customers – she was there, and she rattled them off no problem. So tomorrow we can visit them and see if she's telling the truth."

"I have to work tomorrow."

"When you come home," Martha said. "How many hours do you work, anyway? You hardly have any time for fun stuff." She pouted.

"I know." Pru wondered why she sounded apologetic. "But unfortunately I need to make a living."

"I hear you." Martha nodded. "I used to work nine to five myself – but that was a *long* time ago."

"So who are we going to visit first?" she surprised herself by saying.

"Lemme see." Martha grabbed a notebook from the coffee table. "Brooke, the local hair stylist – make sure you go there when you need a trim." She eyed Pru's auburn locks, and she found herself self-consciously lifting a hand to them.

"She's nice, so I'm glad she's not a suspect, and Mrs. Wagner – although I'm surprised she buys any cosmetics – and Mrs. Finch. What time do you get off work tomorrow?"

"Four again," she replied.

"We'll visit Brooke first, because the salon should still be open, and I don't know where she lives."

"You don't?" Pru said mischievously.

"Ha ha." Martha winked. "But I do know where Mrs. Wagner and Mrs. Finch live, so we can visit them after Brooke."

"This won't be too much for you?" Pru eyed the rolling walker next to Martha.

"My doctor keeps telling me to get a bit more exercise, and Teddy will love going for a walk. One of the good things about this town is everything is pretty close together. And if I get tired from walking to Brooke's, we can come home and jump in your car to finish the rest of the interviews."

"Okay." Pru nodded.

They settled on pizza for dinner, Martha grandly announcing it could be that night instead of tomorrow evening.

When the Hawaiian pizza arrived, Martha allowing Pru to choose the toppings for once, the aroma of red sauce, cheese, ham, and the tanginess of pineapple wafted through the house. Both of them concentrated on eating their share, Pru even hungrier than she thought – maybe it was all the sleuthing talk, as well as a full day at the library?

"That was good." Martha patted her stomach when she'd finished.

"It was." Pru nodded.

Teddy looked hopefully at the empty box on the table.

"I've gotta be good and not give you stuff that could be bad for you." Martha's mouth tilted down. "Sorry, little guy."

"Ruff." Teddy's mouth tilted downward too, then he snuggled his head into the crook of Martha's elbow.

"I'm sure he understands what I'm saying." Martha closed her eyes and snuggled him back, her expression joyful.

"I'm sure he does."

"Ruff!"

CHAPTER 14

The next day, Pru rushed home from work. She was intrigued about meeting Brooke. Remembering how Martha had eyed her hair, she wondered if she should book in for a trim while she was there.

"Let's go!" Martha and Teddy waited on the doorstep for her, decked out in matching turquoise outfits – Martha with her signature style sweatpants and sweater, and Teddy in his turquoise collar and leash.

"Ruff!" Teddy wagged his tail at her, and she bent down to stroke his soft, cotton like fur.

"I can't wait to interview Brooke," Martha said.

They set off down the street, the sun slowly sinking toward the horizon. Martha waved to a few passersby, while Pru held Teddy's lead. The little dog walked happily along the sidewalk, only stopping a few times to sniff interesting blades of grass.

"He's very good on the lead," she observed.

"Isn't he?" Martha grinned. "He's such a well-behaved boy. I'm glad Ed thought of me when he came into the shelter."

"Ed? Oh, the pastry chef at the café."

"That's him." Martha nodded. "He also volunteers at the local animal shelter. He's a good man. And his Danishes are the best. But so are Lauren's cupcakes, and coffee."

"Don't forget the hot chocolate," Pru joked.

"How could I?" Martha chuckled. "But while Teddy and I were waiting for you to come home, we watched a show on TV where they made dog bandanas. Can you sew?" She looked hopefully at Pru.

"Not much."

"Pooh. I've got an old sewing machine – somewhere – and I thought you could make Teddy some.

He'd look real cute wearing one when we go out."

"He would," she agreed.

"They made it look so easy to create one – all you have to do is hem a square of nice fabric."

"Why don't you try making one?" Pru suggested.

"Yeah – maybe I will. If I can find the sewing machine."

"I can set it up for you."

"I guess it will give me something to do when I'm not at the senior center, or the café, or book club." Martha chuckled. "I started that Poirot book last night and Ms. Tobin was right – it's a good story so far."

"I'm hoping to read my copy on the weekend."

"Then we can compare notes and see who guessed the killer first."

"That would be fun." She realized it would be.

They rounded a corner and Martha pointed to the small salon. "There it is. Just down the street from the café."

She cast a longing look at the coffee shop. Another latte would hit the spot right now – and one of their cupcakes – would she ever get the chance to try one? But Martha urged her toward the salon.

Holding the door open for Martha, who trundled inside, she hesitated.

"Are dogs allowed?" She looked down at Teddy, who stared at the hairspray scented interior with big eyes. A woman was getting her hair blow-dried, and another sat in front of a large mirror with wet hair.

"I bet Brooke won't mind." Martha pointed to the door. "I don't see a sign saying they're not."

Pru scanned the glass window as well, but couldn't see anything saying dogs weren't welcome. Taking a deep breath, she followed Martha inside.

A few comfortable looking chairs and a rack of magazines decorated the waiting area. Four stations with large mirrors and a shampoo station made up the rest of the space.

"Yoo hoo, Brooke," Martha called.

A girl around thirty, with chestnut locks featuring attractive reddish highlights, turned off the blow dryer and hurried toward them. She wore black jeans and an emerald sweater.

"Martha." Her eyes widened when she spied the puppy. "Oh, you've brought Teddy." Bending down, she made a fuss of him.

"Hi, I'm Pru." She introduced herself.

"Martha's roommate." Brooke's smile lit up her friendly green eyes. "What can I do for you?"

"We wanted to ask you about buying makeup from Lynda," Martha said.

"And I wondered if I could make an appointment to get my hair trimmed."

"Of course." Brooke nodded and grabbed a large appointment book from the reception desk. "When can you come in?"

"Tomorrow – Saturday?"

"I can squeeze you in at ten."

"Thanks."

"Ooh – you could grab us some cupcakes from the café when you're finished here." Martha's eyes lit up. "The girls close at lunchtime tomorrow."

"Now you're making me hungry," Brooke joked. "I've had appointments all day and only had time for a quick sandwich I brought from home." She glanced back at her two clients. "I need to get back to work in a second – sorry."

"We just wanted to ask you if you bought makeup from Lynda the day Candy was killed," Martha said.

"Candy?"

"The woman who was killed outside the library. She organized a book club but it turned out she was promoting her own book! Pretty clever, huh," Martha said. "Except it wasn't a good book."

"Oh." Brooke's expression cleared. "I did hear a little about that. But I thought Mitch was in charge of the case."

"We're helping," Martha replied grandly. "Because we found her body."

Brooke blanched. "I'm sorry."

"Yeah, me too, but that made me think we should find out whodunnit. Plus we're reading mysteries at book club now – in case I need to pick up any more tips." Martha's tone made it sound like she didn't think she needed much help in that department.

"Lynda's husband Hal is one of the book club members," Pru added. "And we found out that Candy owed Lynda money for cosmetics." She hoped she wasn't being too indiscreet.

"Lynda said we could ask her clients about her whereabouts at the time," Martha put in.

"I see." Brooke nodded. "Yes, I do buy some cosmetics from Lynda – I like to shop local when I can – and she has these really nice lipstick shades." She looked critically at Pru. "I like that pink you're wearing, although I prefer coral shades for myself."

"Oh, yeah." Martha turned to look at Pru. "You're wearing the lipstick I made you buy. It looks nice."

"Thanks." She was more pleased than she thought she should be. It wasn't as if she'd never worn lipstick before.

"Did you buy them from her on—" Martha glanced at Pru. "When was Candy killed?"

"During the second book club, which was two weeks ago."

"What time?" Martha checked.

"In the morning – sometime between ten and eleven. Martha and I found her just after eleven," Pru replied.

"I'll look through my appointment book." Brooke reached behind her and grabbed it, leafing through the pages. "I had a break between appointments around then, but I didn't write down what I did. Usually I go to the café and grab a latte and have a chat with Lauren and Zoe if I have time. So I could have bought some lipstick from Lynda instead." She screwed up her eyes in thought. "I do have a new one I bought from her recently, so it could have been that day."

"Brooke," the woman with the partly blow-dried hair called out, a frown on her face.

"Sorry," Brooke called back. "I'll be there in a sec." She turned to them. "I've got to get back to my clients."

"Of course." Pru nodded. "It was nice meeting you."

"See you tomorrow." Brooke dashed over to her client and turned on the blow dryer.

"Well, pooh," Martha grumbled as they left the salon. "Brooke's not sure one way or the other."

"But it does seem likely that was when she bought a lipstick from Lynda," Pru said.

"Ruff!"

Martha beamed with pride at the fluffy white dog. "Wasn't he a good boy in there?"

"He was," Pru said.

"Although, I don't know why he wasn't sniffing around the corners like Annie does."

"Maybe he doesn't like the way the salon smells?"

"Or maybe because there weren't any clues in there."

"Why would there be clues in Brooke's salon? She's not involved with Candy's death."

"True." Martha nodded. "Which is good. Because where else would I get my hair done?" She touched her springy gray curls. "She knows how to cut my hair which is more than a lot of other hairdressers over the years. So she's got to stay innocent."

She stifled a smile at Martha's logic.

"So who do we visit now? Mrs. Wagner or Mrs. Finch?"

Martha cracked a yawn, hiding it behind her palm. "You're not going to believe this, but I think I need a rest." She looked disgruntled. "I've been looking forward to our sleuthing all day and I wasn't at the senior center for long, either."

"We could go home and use my car," Pru offered.

Martha looked tempted for a second.

"I think I've got to be sensible for once." She made it sound like the worst thing in the world. Then she brightened. "But there's nothing to say we couldn't do a little sleuthing tonight!"

CHAPTER 15

They slowly walked home, Pru making Martha a hot chocolate from the mix she kept in the kitchen and made one for herself.

"Maybe we should stay home tonight." She eyed her roommate. Apart from looking a little tired, Martha seemed okay, but they'd only been living together for a few weeks. Except for using the walker for balance, she didn't know anything about Martha's health.

"I'll be fine." Martha waved away her concern. "Maybe my doctor's right and I do need a bit more exercise – I got plenty today." She chuckled. "But we could take your car tonight when we visit Mrs. Wagner."

"Okay."

Pru made a meatloaf, which Martha gobbled up. "That was good," she praised. "You can make that again."

"Thanks." It was one of her mom's recipes.

"Now we can get going to Mrs. Wagner's."

"It won't be too late to visit?"

"It's only seven-thirty," Martha said. "I bet she'll still be up. Seniors don't go to bed *that* early."

"Sorry," she murmured.

They got into Pru's car, Martha's walker in the trunk. Teddy sat in the back, his eyes bright with curiosity as they drove through the darkened streets.

"Take this left, then this right – no, the next one – then left again – stop!" Martha directed her.

Pru hit the brakes, staring at the small Victorian on the left with a neat front garden.

"We'd better park around the corner," Martha told her. "So she doesn't know we're visiting her."

Pru looked at her. "But we'll be ringing her doorbell. She'll know it's us when she opens the door."

"Yeah, but we shouldn't give her advance notice. We need to surprise her. That way she can't come up with a story to put us off track."

"I thought we were asking Mrs. Wagner to confirm Lynda's alibi."

"We are," Martha replied. "But what if she's in on it with Lynda to kill Candy?"

"Why would she be?" Pru stared at her roommate.

"Maybe Candy owed her money, too."

"For what?"

"That's what we'll have to find out."

With a sigh, Pru drove around the corner. Sometimes Martha's logic defied her – but she couldn't deny that meeting her roommate had definitely added some intrigue to her life.

When she parked around the darkened corner to Martha's satisfaction, she switched off the headlights and ignition.

"Ruff?" Teddy asked, shuffling around on the back seat.

"It's sleuthing time, little guy." Martha turned around to beam at her fur baby. "Isn't this fun?"

"Ruff!" Teddy leaned forward and licked her cheek.

They got out of the car, Pru fetching Martha's walker.

"I wish I didn't have to bother with it," Martha said. "It's a pain sometimes." She clutched the handles. "But at least it gets me places."

They began rounding the corner. They were the only people on the street, and a few stars twinkled above them. A sliver of moon helped light the way as well as the occasional streetlamp.

"Do you think—" Pru started to say in the quiet darkness.

"Shh!" Martha halted her walker and grabbed Pru's arm. "What's that?" She swiveled her head this way and that.

"Where?" Pru looked down at Teddy standing in front of her on the lead. He sniffed the air, and started towing her forward.

"See? Teddy knows."

"Where are we going?" She held onto the leash as Teddy charged forward.

"Ruff!"

"Shh, little guy," Martha cautioned. "We don't want to let them know we're coming!"

Pru scanned the darkened street but couldn't see or hear anyone – or anything. But Teddy's canine instincts were probably more heightened than hers. And Martha's? She wasn't sure if it was her roommate's overactive imagination, or if she'd actually noticed something – or someone – out of the ordinary.

Her eyes widened when she spied a figure dressed in black in front of one of the houses.

"I knew it!" Martha sounded excited. "A burglar!"

"It's someone standing on the sidewalk," she said, although she wondered what they were doing there. Black trousers, black sweater, and a black jacket. The only thing missing was a balaclava over their head.

"No one up to any good would be just loitering like that at this time of night," Martha said.

She checked her watch, surprised to see it was barely eight o'clock. She shivered suddenly in her thin jacket over her lightweight sweater.

"He's writing something down!" Martha nudged her.

Her eyes widened. The figure took out a small notebook and jotted down something as he looked at a car parked nearby on the street.

"Maybe it's Mitch undercover," she suggested.

"Maybe." Martha nodded. "But there's only one way to find out!"

"Martha," Pru called, forgetting to keep her voice down. Her roommate charged down the street.

Teddy nearly pulled her off balance when he followed her.

"Ruff!"

Pru jogged to keep up with the little furball, hoping Martha wasn't going to exhaust herself. What happened to her being tired earlier that evening?

Now she raced full steam ahead with her rolling walker.

"Gotcha!" Martha rammed the stranger in the shins with her walker.

"Ow!" He hopped backwards, stumbled over the sidewalk, and fell down.

"Ruff! Ruff!" Teddy ran around the injured figure.

"Oops," Martha sounded contrite. "I didn't mean to hit you like that. Sometimes I have trouble stopping in time when I'm going full blast, and I was excited. Is that you, Mitch? You're not going to arrest me, are you?"

"No, it's not Mitch," came a muffled reply.

"Then who are you?" Martha reached into her walker seat and pulled out a flashlight, shining it into his face.

The man shielded his eyes from the glaring white beam. "Would you put that away?"

"Sorry – I forgot how bright it was." Martha swung the light to the side, away from everyone's field of vision.

"Are you okay?" Pru spoke. "Are you hurt?"

"No," he replied testily, gingerly getting to his feet. He waved away her offer of help.

Teddy had calmed down and now sniffed the stranger's black boots.

In the dim light, Pru could just make out his features – he appeared to be around thirty, with short, wavy dark hair and a rugged, attractive face.

"Do you always accost strangers like this?" he asked, frowning.

"Of course not," Pru assured him. "I'm sorry. We were going to visit a—" Friend? Suspect? One of Lynda's cosmetic customers?

"—a friend," Martha put in. "We were just strolling along, minding our *own* business, when we saw you and thought you were up to no good, so we decided to investigate."

"Ruff!"

"I see," he said dryly. "Well, how about you visit your friend, and I'll continue with *my* business."

"Which is?" Martha peered at him. "I haven't seen you before, have I? How do I know you're not a bad guy?"

"Because I'm a product of clean living and good intentions?" His eyebrow flickered. "But I think they were right when they said no good deed goes unpunished." He rubbed his shin.

"What are you doing out here?" Pru found her voice. There was something about him that appealed to her – she wasn't sure if it was his good looks, his voice, or his confidence. Perhaps it was all three.

"What are *you* doing out here?" he countered.

"We told you, we're visiting a friend," Martha put in, "and she lives right over there." She pointed to Mrs. Wagner's house on the other side of the street.

"Your turn," Pru said.

"It's a private matter," he finally answered.

"Are you waiting for someone?" Martha asked. "But we saw you writing something down and looking at that car." She pointed to a black sedan parked nearby on the street. "You're a parking inspector!"

"I'm not a parking inspector," he replied a little testily.

A light came on inside the house they stood in front of.

"Now you've done it." He frowned. "You've attracted their attention."

"Whose attention?" Pru stared at him.

"You don't need to know who," he informed her, "but—"

A dark vehicle suddenly pulled to a stop beside them. A tall man got out – and stopped.

"Martha?"

"Mitch!" Martha grinned.

"I was notified of a disturbance."

"Mitch? Is that you?" The stranger stared at him. "They mentioned a Mitch but I didn't think they meant you."

"Jesse?" Mitch's face broke into a smile and they did the whole guy backslapping thing. "What are you doing here? I thought you were still working in Sacramento."

"I was, but I didn't see eye to eye with the new boss, so I decided to take some of the leave I'd accrued," he said. "I'm doing a private job right now – for my cousin. She thinks her husband is cheating on her while she's out of town."

"He's not a burglar?" Martha sounded disappointed.

The front door of the house opened and a man in his forties walked out wearing a gray robe. "Officer, this man has been lurking outside my house, and I want to know why."

"It's Detective," Mitch informed him.

"Do you think you should go out there?" A shrill female voice suddenly sounded, then a woman dressed in tight jeans and a black, low-cut blouse hurried after him.

"That is definitely not my cousin," Jesse muttered.

"Jesse?" The homeowner blanched. "What are you doing here? Oh, no!" His head swiveled to the woman behind him, back to Jesse, and then onto Mitch, Martha, and Pru.

"Gotcha," Jesse said in satisfaction.

CHAPTER 16

After Mitch advised Jesse's cousin-in-law to go back inside and sort out his domestic matters, the two guys started talking about old times in the police department at Sacramento.

"This is real exciting." Martha tapped her foot. "But we were going to visit Mrs. Wagner and now it's getting late. Pru has to go to work in the morning."

"Sorry, Martha," Mitch replied. "You two go on with whatever you're doing."

"Are you sure about that?" Jesse rubbed his shin again and looked at Martha wryly. "She's a demon with that walker."

"Don't I know it," Mitch said ruefully. "But I'm sure she didn't do it on purpose."

"I already said I didn't," Martha said. "But maybe you shouldn't have been loitering when the senior sleuthing club was busy in the area."

"The what?" Mitch stared at her. "The senior sleuthing—"

"Club," Martha said proudly. "And all of us are right here. Me, Teddy, and Pru."

"Ruff!"

"You don't look old enough to be a senior," Jesse murmured to her, scrutinizing her appearance.

Pru found herself blushing and hoped he couldn't tell in the dim light. "Thanks. I think."

"Since I'm the president, I get to decide who's in," Martha continued. "And since I'm a senior, it's obvious it should be called the senior sleuthing club."

"That makes sense – sort of," Mitch muttered.

"We're busy on the case of Candy's murder. Since you haven't solved it yet, Mitch, we've decided to do some digging around. When we catch the killer, we'll let you know."

Jesse looked like he was trying not to laugh.

"I'll have you know that we've already discovered some pertinent information," Pru told him, for some reason wanting to wipe the smile off his face.

"If you find out anything, make sure you tell me," Mitch advised.

"Mrs. Wagner was a cosmetic customer of Lynda's," Martha said. "That's who we're gonna visit now."

Mitch blinked. "I see." He turned to Pru. "Make sure Martha doesn't overdo it."

"I'll try."

Martha snorted. "I'm a grown woman who doesn't need a babysitter. Come on, Pru!" She charged across the street.

"Ruff!" Teddy towed Pru after her.

"The senior sleuthing club," she heard Jesse laugh after them. "Now I've heard everything."

"You don't know the half of it," Mitch said.

They reached the other side of the deserted street safely. A light shone in Mrs. Wagner's house.

"Are you sure it's not too late now?" Pru murmured as Martha negotiated her way to the porch. "It must be after nine."

"But there's a light on, so she hasn't gone to bed yet." Martha rang the doorbell. "Yoo hoo, it's Martha." She turned to Pru. "That's so she knows it's safe to open the door. Us seniors have to be careful."

The front door opened. An older woman peered out. Spectacles perched on her slightly beaky nose, and her gray hair was cut in a feathered style. "Martha? What are you doing here? And at this hour! I was just about to go to bed."

"Sorry to disturb you so late." Martha turned and glared at Mitch and Jesse still talking to each other across the street. "We got delayed. You probably know that we're looking into Candy's murder, and we wanted to know if you bought makeup from Lynda on the day Candy was killed, which was—" she glanced at Pru.

"Two weeks and two days ago."

"Looking into whose murder?" Mrs. Wagner frowned.

"Candy. You know, the woman who died outside the library," Martha informed her.

"Oh." Mrs. Wagner's expression cleared. "I did hear something about a woman getting killed there." She shuddered. "Just when you think a library is one of the safest places you could be. But how do you know I bought cosmetics from Lynda?"

"She told us," Martha said. "She's happy for us to verify her alibi."

"It wasn't for myself, of course," Mrs. Wagner said. "I don't hold with all these painted faces. It was for my niece, and I know Lynda is doing it to supplement her income." She shook her head. "It's not like we get much money these days. Every little bit helps."

"It sure does," Martha replied. "That's why Pru here is my new roomie."

"I heard something about that." Mrs. Wagner nodded. "I hope you've got a job, young lady, and you're paying your way."

"I'm the assistant librarian," she replied.

"I certainly hope you didn't have anything to do with that woman's death." Mrs. Wagner eyed her askance.

"Of course she didn't," Martha said impatiently. "Me and Pru found Candy's body together. And Pru is a real good roomie."

"Thanks." Pru smiled.

"Ruff!"

"See, Teddy thinks so too."

Mrs. Wagner's expression softened slightly at the sight of the white puppy.

"Did you happen to buy cosmetics from Lynda on Wednesday two weeks ago?" Pru asked. She stifled a yawn.

"If Lynda says that was the day, it probably was," Mrs. Wagner replied. "She gave me a receipt, but I can't remember where I put it." She frowned.

"Brooke didn't mention getting a receipt. Huh." Martha frowned.

"Maybe she didn't think of it," Pru suggested. "It might be crumpled up in her purse."

"Good thinking." Martha nodded. "Yeah, that's probably it. And if Lynda is giving out receipts, then we can double check later that everything tallies for that day. Unless …"

"Unless?" Pru asked.

"What if she kept some blank receipts to give herself an alibi? She could have filled them out after and backdated them!" Martha looked excited.

"Why, Martha, I don't know how you can reason like that," Mrs. Wagner chided. "Anyone would think you were a criminal mastermind."

Martha's eyes lit up. "I think that's one of the best compliments I've ever received. Thanks!"

"Ruff!"

"See, Teddy thinks it's a good one, too."

"I guess we'll have to tally the receipts from Lynda's book with the customers' on that day," Pru said.

"Yeah. Tomorrow."

"Was there anything else you wanted, Martha?" Mrs. Wagner sounded a little impatient. "I have a doctor's appointment early tomorrow morning and I need to go to bed."

"Sorry. Thanks for your help."

They turned to leave, the front door making a click behind them.

"I think we should go to bed, too." Pru couldn't help the yawn that escaped.

"I guess." Martha sighed. "If it wasn't for those two – two – over there, we could have visited Mrs. Finch as well. Maybe. But it's much too late now."

Pru glanced across the street. Jesse and Mitch were still standing on the sidewalk, talking as if they were never going to stop. She told herself to forget all about Jesse. She had plenty of other things to think about right now – her new job, sleuthing with Martha and Teddy, and making sure she read *The Mysterious Affair at Styles* in time for book club next week.

***

"Look what I found!" Martha called to her the next morning as she left the bathroom.

"What is it?" She peered into Martha's bedroom.

"My sewing machine!" Martha was already dressed in a fuchsia sweatpants and matching sweater, and her closet door was open, with half the items pulled out and sitting on the floor. "Now I can make Teddy a bandana!"

"Ruff!" Teddy pawed through some of the tossed clothing, looking for treasure.

"Do you have any fabric you can use?"

"I found a stash buried at the bottom of the closet." Martha grinned. "It's plain old red, but I think it will look cute on him." She held up a wrinkled mass of scarlet fabric.

"I can move the sewing machine for you."

"Goody. I was hoping you'd say that." Martha nodded. "We can put it on the dining table."

Pru bent her knees and picked up the old black machine. Luckily, it wasn't as heavy as it looked.

"How long have you had this?" she puffed, carrying it to the dining area.

"Probably fifty years. But it worked okay last time I used it."

After setting it up on the table, Pru looked at the pile of fabric. "You might have to iron that before you try to make Teddy's bandana."

"Pooh. Ironing is boring." Martha wrinkled her nose. Then she looked down at Teddy, who stared at the sewing machine in fascination. "But I bet Teddy would like it if I ironed it for him. I don't want him walking around with a crumpled scarf."

"Ruff!"

After finishing a quick breakfast of fiber-filled cereal, she said goodbye to the two of them and headed for Brooke's salon.

She decided to walk the few blocks, her thoughts turning to Candy's death.

Who could the killer be if it wasn't someone from book club who killed Candy? Just the thought of someone in that little group being a murderer made her shiver.

Was it suspicious that Hal didn't turn up at book club that week, but his wife Lynda did instead? The other members had been there.

And what about Martha's theory that Lynda could have doctored some of her cosmetic receipts? Surely she would be found out if they checked the stubs with the receipts held by the customers?

Pru reached the salon and spent a pleasant time chatting to Brooke as she worked her magic on her hair, deliberately not thinking or talking about Candy's demise. When the cape was whisked off, Pru stared at her auburn strands. Brooke had kept the same style but added some texture here and there.

"I love it." She smiled at herself in the mirror.

"Good." Brooke's smile met hers. "Have you tried Lauren's cupcakes yet?"

"I'm just about to. Martha's ordered me to bring some home."

"Martha is a real livewire." Brooke chuckled. "But I'm glad you've moved in with her. Rentals are so hard to find around here."

"It's scary," Pru agreed.

When she paid at the register, she thought to ask, "Did Lynda give you a receipt for the lipstick you bought from her recently?"

"Yes. I'm sure she did." Brooke looked through her purse behind the counter. "Let's see. No, no, no, – maybe – no, no, here it is!" She held up a crumpled receipt. "It has the date on it, too." She read out the date which was the day of Candy's murder.

"It doesn't have the time on it, does it?" she asked hopefully.

Brooke scanned the piece of paper. "No. Just the date, my name, and the name of the lipstick shade."

"Thanks." She said goodbye to Brooke, and walked down the street to the café.

The place was packed, and after saying hello to Annie, the Norwegian Forest Cat hostess, and explaining she wanted to grab some cupcakes to go, it was her turn to order.

"Hi, Lauren." She smiled at the cupcake extraordinaire. Her eyes widened at the treats on display. "I think I'll have one of each. They all look so good."

"Thanks." Lauren smiled. "That's one red velvet, one mocha, and one super vanilla. How's Martha?"

"She's busy making a bandana for Teddy."

"Ohh. I can't wait to see it on him. How's—" she glanced this way and that, but her cousin Zoe was wiping down a table at the back "—the sleuthing going?"

"We've made a little progress," she replied.

"I heard about your night out." Lauren giggled. "Mitch couldn't stop talking about it – and how he discovered his old friend was here. He, Jesse, and Zoe's husband, Chris, are getting together tonight for pizza. It will be good for him to relax a little."

Pru paid for the cupcakes and waved goodbye to Lauren and Annie, watching for a moment as Annie led a customer to a rare vacant table. She'd never seen such a thing before.

Although the assistant librarian position had been the only one she'd been offered, she was glad she'd taken it. She was starting to think that maybe she'd be able to fit into Gold Leaf Valley, and leave the past behind.

Stepping out into the street, she blinked as a tall figure bumped into her. Clutching the box of treats, she stared up at ... Jesse.

"What are you doing here?" she blurted out.

"I could ask you the same thing." His smile crinkled across his mouth.

"Buying some goodies?" He looked even better that morning in faded blue jeans and a black sweater.

She felt herself flush. "For your information, the senior sleuthing club needs some fortification."

"Discovered the killer yet?"

"Not quite," Pru told him.

A couple of people walked past on the sidewalk, one woman dressed in a smart suit.

"Why don't you let Mitch do his job? He's pretty good at it."

"Then why hasn't the killer been caught?"

Jesse frowned. "There are a lot of things that go on during an investigation. Trust me, Mitch is homing in on the killer."

"Did he tell you that?"

"He didn't need to. I used to work with him back in Sacramento. You and your senior friend need to let him do his job."

"Her name is Martha, and she's my roommate. And she's had some pretty good ideas about investigating Candy's death."

"If you say so." He shook his head. "I don't know why you think you can be a detective when you work in a library."

"How about you? You were lurking in the street trying to catch a cheating husband."

"And I caught him." He smiled. "That's what happens to cheaters – they eventually get caught."

She took a step back.

"Are you okay?" He looked at her closely.

"I'm fine," she managed. "I've got to go – Martha's waiting."

She hurried down the street, wondering why she let his comment about cheaters bother her so much. She wasn't one – and her family knew that. That's all that should matter.

***

"Ruff!" *Look!* Teddy greeted her at the door, wearing a slightly rumpled red bandana around his neck.

195

"Don't you look handsome?" Pru bent down and gave him a scratch behind his ears.

"Ruff!" Teddy's mouth seemed to smile.

"Is that you, Pru?" Martha called from down the hallway.

"Yes." She followed Teddy to the living room. Martha slumped on the sofa. A few red bandanas were piled next to her.

"I'm pooped from sewing." Martha pointed to the crumpled bandanas. "It took me ages while you were out to make a half decent one. You were right about ironing them. I ironed Teddy's three times—" she pointed to the fabric around the puppy's neck "—before it looked good enough for him to wear."

"You've done a great job." Pru picked up a bandana from the pile. Three of the corners were very wonky. She grabbed another one. Two corners were wonky and one was somehow caught up at the back and sewn onto the bottom half.

"See?" Martha pouted. "I'm sure I was better at sewing twenty years ago – not that I've ever done that much."

"But you ended up making a decent one for Teddy," Pru tried to cheer her up.

"Yeah." Martha smiled. "But I think I need a bit of a rest before we visit Mrs. Finch today." She sighed.

"Don't forget I've got to read that book for next week."

"Oh, yeah. I stayed up late reading more of it last night," Martha said. "I was only going to read a few pages, but somehow I was still glued to it thirty minutes later." She yawned. "I'd better not do that tonight."

Pru folded up the other bandanas. "Where would you like these?"

"In the trash?" Martha joked. "I guess I'd better put them back in my closet. I hope Teddy keeps that bandana nice and clean, because it's the only one that's wearable."

CHAPTER 17

Martha admired Pru's hair, and then declared they should have cupcakes for lunch.

She couldn't resist, and they munched away at the dining table, after Teddy got his own lunch of kibble.

"Mmm," Martha mumbled, eating half a super vanilla. They'd decided to split each treat so they could try each flavor.

"These are good," Pru agreed, eyeing her last half which was red velvet. She popped a small piece into her mouth – the red cake crumb, flavored with cocoa and a hint of vanilla, combined with the tangy flavor of the cream cheese frosting, was a delicious explosion of baked goodness.

"Told you." Martha grinned, her mouth sticky with icing. "Okay, after we've finished these, we should visit

Mrs. Finch. I feel revived now. And then you can read your book, and we can see who guessed the killer first!"

"Good idea." Pru nodded. "Oh – I asked Brooke today if she received a receipt from Lynda for her lipstick, and she found it in her purse."

"I knew it couldn't be Brooke," Martha said in satisfaction. "Goody."

"Maybe this means it couldn't be Lynda as well."

"That's true, but we should still doublecheck the receipts. What other suspects do we have? Hal, Eleanor, and Doris."

"What about Ms. Tobin? She's in the book club."

Martha stared at her in shock. "It can't be Ms. Tobin because she's my friend and she would never murder anyone. She might tell you off if you upset her, but kill someone?" She shook her head. "I can't imagine it."

"Okay." Pru backed off, although she thought they shouldn't discount anyone right now. But she didn't like seeing Martha upset. "What about Hal? He could have killed Candy because he was angry that she owed Lynda money for her cosmetics."

"Ooh – what about Gary? From the burger diner? Because he had to take over cooking Candy's burger since she wasn't happy with Doris's efforts, and ended up giving it to her for free!"

Pru glanced at her. "But wouldn't he be used to comping a meal occasionally for a difficult customer?"

"Yeah, I guess that probably happens," Martha finally agreed. "And of course I don't want it to be him – because what would happen to his diner? There aren't a lot of places to eat around here, and his is one of the best. I bet it would be even one of the best in LA or New York!"

"You could be right." Her burger and fries had been delicious, and not too expensive.

"I guess you're correct – Hal has a bigger motive than Gary," Martha continued. "Because of Candy owing Lynda money. Maybe he got so angry about it that he killed her after book club, just like you said."

"Maybe he bumped into her outside and asked her to pay up and when she refused he became enraged and lost his temper," Pru suggested.

"Yeah!" Martha pointed her finger at her. "That sounds good. Hmm. Maybe I should add something like that to my retired lady detective script. I haven't tinkered with it much lately, because I've been too busy doing some real-life sleuthing."

"Ruff!" Teddy hopped up on the chair next to Martha.

"Wait until Mrs. Finch sees you in your bandana," Martha told him. "I bet she'll love to see you looking so smart."

Teddy licked Martha's cheek.

"See? I'm sure he knows exactly what I'm saying," Martha marveled.

"I think he does," Pru admitted.

They finished their sweet treats lunch, and then got ready to visit Mrs. Finch.

"Should we take my car?" Pru eyed Martha. Her roommate had done quite a bit of sleuthing lately –

perhaps they should be lazy and drive this afternoon.

"Yeah – why not?" Martha agreed. "We can go for a walk tomorrow."

"Ruff!" Teddy's brown eyes lit up at the word.

They finished getting ready and set off in Pru's car.

"This way, then turn left, then right, then left," Martha instructed. "Mrs. Finch lives around the corner from the café, so it's not far."

"That's handy."

"Yeah. I wish I lived that close!" Martha chuckled. "Look! There's Hal!" Martha pointed at a figure walking along the sidewalk. "We'd better stop and talk to him."

"What are we going to say?"

"We can ask him if he killed Candy and judge his reaction," Martha told her. "That's what they do in some of these detective novels."

Pru pulled over and switched off the ignition.

"Yoo hoo, Hal!" Martha got out of the car without waiting for her walker.

"Ruff?" Teddy pressed his face to the back window, watching the two of them.

"We'd better go after her." Pru snapped on his lead and helped him out. She kept an eye on Martha, but her roommate seemed steady on her feet.

"Hi, Martha," she heard Hal say. He wore dark trousers and a blue sweater. "What are you doing out here?"

"I could ask you the same thing," Martha said. "We're visiting a friend nearby. I saw you and thought I'd stop and say hello. Have you finished reading the Agatha Christie for book club next week?"

"What Agatha Christie?" He frowned. "Lynda's been reading some book, but she hasn't been talking about it much."

"Aha!" Martha crowed.

"Aha what?" His frown deepened. "I don't think I'll come to book club next week anyway, if Lynda's going. It's good sometimes for a couple to have separate interests, and reading has never been much of mine."

"That's a shame," Pru spoke. "I thought you were enjoying the group."

Teddy tugged on the lead and sniffed Hal's sneakers.

"It wasn't bad," he admitted, "apart from that first book we had to read, but I'd rather spend some time with my brother, or visit the senior center and see if some of my friends are there. And sometimes I felt as if your boss was spying on us. I'd feel a prickle at the back of my neck, and if I turned my head, there she was staring at me from her big desk."

"I think she was just trying to keep an eye on things." Pru wondered if any of the other members had noticed her boss's way of keeping tabs on the group, although she'd wondered at the time if her boss had been keeping tabs on *her*.

"I thought it was a bit creepy," Hal replied. "Lynda can come in my place."

"If you change your mind, you'll be very welcome," she told him.

"Thanks." He nodded. "I wish you were the head librarian instead of Barbara. She doesn't exactly make you feel at ease in there."

"I bet Pru will be a big head librarian one day," Martha declared. "Just you wait and see!"

"Ruff!"

"Thanks." She smiled at the three of them.

Hal continued on his way, leaving Martha staring after him.

"Pooh – I forgot to ask him if he killed Candy."

She had visions of Martha running after Hal – with or without her walker – to do just that.

"Why don't we see Mrs. Finch first? And then we can decide whether to visit Hal and ask him that question," Pru suggested.

"Good idea." Martha beamed. "I knew I made the right decision making you a senior sleuthing club member!"

They got into the car and drove the rest of the way to Mrs. Finch's. Martha directed her to park outside a sweet, cream Victorian with a neat lawn.

They knocked on the door. An elderly lady opened it, her gray hair in a slightly untidy bun. She wore a sage green skirt and white blouse, and peered at them through delicate pink spectacles.

"Hi, Mrs. Finch!" Martha grinned. "Ruff!"

"Oh, my, look at you, Teddy." Mrs. Finch smiled down at the puppy. "Did you make that sweet bandana, Martha?"

"I did," Martha replied proudly. "This morning."

"I bet Teddy loves wearing it."

"Ruff!" *I do!*

"This is Pru," Martha introduced her. "She's my new roomie and fellow sleuth, along with Teddy. We're gonna solve Candy's murder!"

"You'd better come in."

They followed Mrs. Finch down the oatmeal and lilac hall to the living room, which featured beige carpeting and a fawn lounge suite.

"What can I do for you?" Mrs. Finch settled in one of the arm chairs and gestured for them to do the same.

Pru sat on the opposite sofa, the cushion next to her sinking as Martha joined her; Teddy sitting neatly on the carpet in front of Martha.

"What a good boy he is," Mrs. Finch praised. "You've done a wonderful job with him, Martha."

"Thanks." Martha grinned. "But I can't take all the credit – whoever had him before me plus the volunteers at the shelter did all the work. He's been so good since I adopted him."

"Ruff!"

The three of them chuckled.

"We wanted to ask you about buying makeup from Lynda," Pru ventured.

"That's right." Martha nodded. "We've got a theory that Lynda could have killed Candy – you know, the woman who died outside the library a couple of weeks ago – and we need to check her alibi. Lynda said she sold cosmetics to you, Brooke, and Mrs. Wagner on the day in question."

"Yes, I did hear about a lady called Candy being killed. And that she was an author?"

"Yes." Pru explained about Candy being in their book club, and that she was actually the author of the first book they read, but had kept it a secret.

"Oh, my." Mrs. Finch shook her head. "Well, I do buy a bit of makeup from Lynda, but I'm afraid I have no idea where I put the receipt."

"Did you buy some from her two and a half weeks ago?" Pru asked.

"Well, now, let me see." Mrs. Finch closed her eyes and tilted her head back. "It could have been around that time. I know I bought a new pink lipstick from her, but I haven't worn it yet, because I wanted to use up my old color first."

"Is that what you're wearing now?" Martha asked.

"It's very nice," Pru complimented.

"Thank you, dear." Mrs. Finch opened her eyes and smiled. "Yes, it's my old color, but I'm afraid I just bought the same shade as it's my favorite."

"Pru bought a lipstick from Lynda as well." Martha turned to her and frowned. "You're not wearing it."

"I was in a hurry," she replied.

"I'm sorry I can't be specific about the date, Martha," Mrs. Finch said.

"That's okay," Martha replied. "Maybe Lynda was telling the truth after all, and she's not the killer."

"I sincerely hope not," Mrs. Finch remarked.

After a few minutes of chit-chat, they said goodbye to Mrs. Finch, Martha promising to tell her when they caught the killer.

"Who should we question now?" Martha pondered as they walked down the little garden path to Pru's car. "Maybe we'd better go to Hal and Lynda's house and I'll ask him if he killed Candy and watch his reaction."

Pru blinked – there was a piece of white paper on the windshield.

"Did you get a ticket?" Martha glanced at the note tucked under the wiper blade. "I bet it was that guy

Jesse – he's a parking inspector after all!"

She gingerly pulled out the paper from the wiper blade and unfolded it. Graceful handwriting in black ink stated:

Meet me behind the library at four o'clock today if you want to find out about Candy.

"Ooh!" Martha's face lit up. "Someone wants to give us valuable information about Candy's killer! What's the time?"

Pru glanced at her watch. "Three-thirty."

"Goody. Plenty of time to get to the library."

"Ruff!" Teddy had been nosing around the car wheels. He trotted up to Martha and spat out a small metal buckle.

"Whatcha got?" Martha started to bend down, but Pru beat her to it.

"Maybe it's from a belt buckle? Or a shoe?" It looked oddly familiar but she couldn't place it.

"Good boy," Martha praised. "I bet it's a clue. Now you're finding clues just like Annie does!"

"Ruff!" *Goody!*

"We just have to find someone walking around with an unfastened belt or a shoe without its buckle." Martha blinked. "What about Hal? Did he wear a belt today?"

"I don't think so," she answered slowly, trying to remember Hal's outfit. "Dark trousers and a blue sweater – that's what he was wearing before we visited Mrs. Finch."

"You're right," Martha replied after a moment. "Yeah. But was he wearing a belt with those trousers?"

Pru closed her eyes and tried to picture Hal. "I don't think so," she replied slowly.

"Pooh. Because if he was, he could have been the person leaving the note for us."

"Ruff!"

"Let's go to the library." Martha trundled around to the trunk and looked expectantly at Pru. "We don't want to be late!"

CHAPTER 18

"Are you sure this is a good idea?" Pru asked a few minutes later. She'd just parked in the deserted library lot.

"Of course it is," Martha replied confidently. "There are three of us, anyway. If this person turns out to be dangerous, I bet we can defeat him – or her."

"Let's hope it doesn't come to that," Pru said. "I think we should turn on our cell phones now, in case we need to call for help."

"Good idea." Martha rummaged in her pockets. "Oh. I think mine's in the basket of my walker."

"I've got mine." Pru pulled it out of her purse and switched it on. "There. All ready."

They got out of the car, Pru fetching Martha's walker from the trunk. She snapped on Teddy's lead – the puppy looked eager and ready for action.

"I wonder why they wanted to meet behind the building," she mused. "The library is closed this afternoon, so why not meet in the parking lot, if this is on the up and up?"

"Maybe they don't want to be seen," Martha said sagely. "Maybe they've got a lot to lose if someone walking or driving past sees them talking to us."

"But how would a passerby know what we're talking about with this person?"

"What if this passerby knows what this note leaving person knows?" Martha tapped the side of her nose. "Don't forget, Gold Leaf Valley is a small town. Lots of people know lots of other people's business. Especially if you hang out at the senior center – like Hal."

"Do you still think Hal left this note?" Pru unfolded it and read it again, noting the elegant script.

"I think there's a good chance he did." Martha nodded. "And I bet he knows who the killer is!"

They walked around to the back of the building, Pru wondering if this was such a good idea, after all. The place was deserted, and there had been very little traffic driving past when they'd parked in the lot.

At least they weren't meeting the person who left the note in the same spot where they'd found Candy's body.

"Martha, do you think—" she drew in a deep breath, her eyes widening when she saw the person standing behind the library.

"Eleanor! What are you doing here?" Martha frowned. "We've come to meet someone for a secret meeting, so if you don't mind, would you like to stand around somewhere else?"

"I *am* your secret meeting." Eleanor didn't sound amused. She looked quite severe in her smart suit, and her classically elegant handbag hung over the crook of her elbow.

"Really, Martha, I don't think you realize how you sound at times. What if I'd just been out for a stroll and was standing here admiring the trees?" Eleanor pointed to a few red maples behind her. "And you're asking me to run along?"

"I guess I didn't think about that," Martha mumbled. "Sorry."

"Your note said you had information about Candy," Pru put in.

"Ruff!" Teddy leaped forward, nearly pulling Pru off her feet. He sniffed Eleanor's shoes, and then her leg.

Eleanor stepped back. "Get your dog under control," she ordered.

"Sorry." Pru asked Teddy to heel, which he did so reluctantly.

"Good boy." Martha beamed down at him. "Now, what's this super-secret information you have for us about Candy?"

"I realize you've been looking into the case," Eleanor replied. "Exactly how far have you gotten?"

"We're looking at Hal being the killer," Martha replied. "Or his wife, Lynda. Because Candy owed her money for cosmetics. Now it's your turn."

Eleanor smiled. "You're definitely on the right track. I'm sure it's Hal or Lynda as well. I just don't understand why the police haven't arrested them yet. I think you and Pru have done more investigating than Detective Denman." She shook her head.

"Ruff?" Teddy leapt forward and stood on his hind legs, sniffing Eleanor's purse. He patted a paw on the vintage leather.

Pru's eyes widened as she noticed one of the three decorative metal buckles missing on the handbag. She frantically unzipped her own purse and felt around for the hard metal object. Her heart hammering, she pulled it out and held it up.

"This is yours."

"Is that the buckle?" Martha squinted.

"It's from Eleanor's handbag."

"Ruff!" *Yes!* Teddy jumped around in a circle and trotted back to Pru.

"Of course it's not," Eleanor blustered. "This purse is a work of art and was very, very expensive when I bought it."

"Yeah – it *is* her buckle." Martha nodded. "Even I can see that. It must have come off when you left the note on Pru's car. And your handbag is nice, but it looks pretty old."

"You can't get good workmanship like this anymore." Eleanor patted her purse protectively.

"You're probably right," Pru agreed. "You always look so well turned out and elegant." She glanced down at Eleanor's shoes – the faded leather shiny and well-polished, but showing its age a little.

"Thank you." Eleanor nodded. "I do try to keep up appearances – they're so important, don't you think? Unfortunately, my investments haven't been doing well for a while now, which is why I had to downsize and move to that new subdivision on the way to Sacramento."

"I bet it's still fancier than my little duplex," Martha commented. "Oh well, I guess you get used to living a certain way."

"Yes, you do," Eleanor agreed crisply. Shading her eyes from the sun, she took a step to the side.

"Watch out!" Pru noticed a bucket next to her foot. She hadn't spotted it before – but then the sun hadn't been shining directly on it a few minutes ago.

"Not another bucket of water!" Eleanor's foot froze in mid-air. "I definitely don't want to get my shoes wet, not like when I argued with Candy—" Her hand flew to her mouth when she realized what she'd just uttered.

"It was you!" Martha pointed an accusing finger at Eleanor. "You killed Candy! How else would you know about the bucket of water being there?"

"Did you throw it over her head?" Pru asked.

"Yes, it was me!" Eleanor's eyes suddenly blazed. "And that stupid person who left that water lying around – probably a gardener – should be fired. I got my shoes wet when I poured the water over

Candy's head. If the bucket hadn't been there, I wouldn't have bothered, but I was sick of hearing how her character Melisande loved the ocean. That's all Candy droned on about."

"Why did you kill her?" Pru furrowed her brow. "Surely not because you disliked *Race to the Sunset*?"

"I can't believe that bilge got published," Eleanor bit out. "Even if it was a small press run by her brother-in-law!"

"Huh?" Martha's mouth parted. "Are you saying a family member published her book?"

"Yes, that's exactly what I'm saying." Eleanor fisted her hands on her hips. "Unbelievable, isn't it? It just goes to show that nepotism is still alive and well!"

"Lynda mentioned seeing you at a writer's group years ago," Pru said, her eyes widening. "Were you in the same group as Candy?"

"Good one." Martha grinned. "See? You can do this sleuthing thing."

"Yes," Eleanor replied. "At times she worked on that terrible Melisande story back then. Every week we had to listen to her drone on and on, and then we had to listen to everyone else drone on and on about their own books. How was that going to help me with mine? So when I saw her at book club, I couldn't believe it! And then, when she was so insistent on reading *Race to the Sunset* – although her manuscript had a different title back then – and she mentioned Melisande, I knew it was the same story from the writing group."

"So that's why you were a little snarky with her at times," Pru said.

"Yes. And you know what the worst thing was? She didn't even remember me! She treated me like a stranger at book club."

"But didn't Lynda remember her from the writing group?" Martha wanted to know.

"Lynda only came one time as far as I can remember, and that was the week Candy didn't show up. At least we got a break from hearing about boring Melisande that time."

"If her book is so bad, how did it get published?" Martha asked.

"Because the small press publisher is her brother-in-law," Eleanor replied. "Our writing group was aware of this small press – our teacher told us about it – but none of us realized at the time that Candy was related to the man who owned it. When my manuscript was finally ready to submit, I was confident it would be accepted by this publisher. I couldn't believe it when it was rejected! A couple of other ladies in the group also had their manuscripts rejected as well. And then one day Candy waltzes in and says her story was accepted. That was the first of her Becky Blanche novels.

"I don't know why it took so long to publish *Race to the Sunset* – I checked the copyright page on my book club copy and it was only published a few months ago. So maybe the story was just as bad as I thought it was all those years ago, and it's taken her this long to get it into a satisfactory state." Eleanor snorted. "Not that *I* would call it satisfactory."

"What about your own writing?" Pru asked. "Have you kept at it?"

"No." Eleanor shook her head. "Because a while later another member in the writing group said she'd heard from someone that Candy was related to that small press publisher and that's why we all got rejected. He only had one slot left and his wife, who is Candy's sister, nagged him to publish Candy's book. So if I can't even get published with a small-time publisher, how would I get published by a big publisher? Not long after, I left the group, and stopped writing. What was the point?"

"I'm sorry," Pru replied. She could tell from the hurt tone in Eleanor's voice that she hadn't gotten over that rejection.

"But why did you kill Candy?" Martha frowned.

"Because I got into an argument with her," Eleanor replied. "That day when she stormed out of book club, I found her stomping around outside the library. I went up to her and couldn't help myself – I told her how bad *Race to the Sunset* was and I was sick of hearing about Melisande *again*. And you know what? *She didn't even remember me from that writing group, even though we both attended for over a year!*

"If it hadn't been for her, her brother-in-law might have published *my* book. So when she pushed me, saying I'm not allowed to say anything bad about *her* book, I pushed her back. Somehow I ended up shoving her against the brick wall, and she banged her head and fell down. I was so angry, I grabbed that bucket of water and tossed it in her face. Then I left."

"You didn't check if she was alive?" Pru asked, shocked.

"I thought she was just unconscious," Eleanor replied. "It was all her fault in the first place, anyway. If she hadn't cheated and used her connections to get published, I wouldn't have gotten mad at her."

"I'm gonna have to call Mitch," Martha said after a moment.

"Ruff!" *Yes!* Teddy stood on his hind legs and patted the side of the walker basket.

"That's right, I left my phone in there." Martha nodded.

"Mine's turned on." Pru pulled it out of her purse.

"Stop right there!" Eleanor had her hand in her bag. "I've got a gun in here and I'm not afraid to use it."

"It doesn't look like a gun to me." Martha squinted at the elegant old purse. "I think it's just your finger making a pointy motion." She turned on her phone.

"Wait!" There was an edge of desperation in Eleanor's voice. "Don't you want to know who your roommate really is?"

"Pru Armstrong, assistant librarian," Martha replied, puzzled. "Everyone knows that."

"But do you know she was nearly kicked out of college *for cheating*?"

Pru gasped, and took a step back. "How do you know that?"

"Ruff?" Teddy trotted over to her and nuzzled his face against her leg. She bent down to stroke him.

"Pru's not a cheater," Martha said hotly. "She's a good girl, although she can get a little bossy at times with being neat and tidy. And she should wear lipstick more often if she wants to catch a hottie."

"Would you like to explain, Prudence Armstrong?" Eleanor asked archly.

She paled as Eleanor, Martha, and Teddy looked at her, Martha and Teddy wearing enquiring expressions.

"It's true," she choked out, "but I wasn't the cheater. It was my best friend – well, I thought she was my best friend, until she copied my answers on our last big exam and when she was found out, tried to blame it all on me."

"Ha! I knew you were a good girl," Martha said triumphantly. "Phew. You *nearly* had me going for a minute,

Eleanor." She wrapped an arm around Pru's shoulders. "Us roomies have to stick together."

"Ruff!" *Yes!*

"Thanks, Martha." She smiled gratefully at her new friend. "But how did you know?" Pru turned to Eleanor.

"I asked your boss Barbara about you, because I didn't like you nosing around. Don't worry, I told her I thought you were doing a good job running book club, and my niece – not that I have one – was interested in becoming a librarian and I'd wondered where you'd gone to college. When she told me, I called the college pretending I was a prospective employer, and I got a very chatty receptionist who told me all about your cheating scandal."

Pru's mouth parted.

"So that's why you didn't get any other job offers," Martha tsked. "If all the librarians called the college and got that same receptionist, that would put them off hiring you."

"It must be." She nodded. "I applied to so many libraries all over the country – I wanted to get away from Colorado after what happened, although my family believed me, and my professor spoke up for me. I'd always gotten good grades, while my friend partied a lot and was late with her assignments, and didn't do very well on exams. This library was the only one that offered me an interview, and then a job. So they mustn't have spoken to that receptionist."

"I'm glad," Martha said, "because otherwise we wouldn't have met." She beamed at Pru, who couldn't help smiling back.

"This is all very touching," Eleanor said harshly, "but I still have the problem of you two knowing what happened with Candy."

"Ruff!" *Three!*

"That's right, Teddy." Martha glanced down at him. "There's three of us."

Eleanor rolled her eyes. "The first thing I'll do when I get out of here is sell Teddy. Dogs should be seen and not heard. I'll pass him off as some rare breed and might be able to make a couple of thousand dollars."

"He *is* a rare breed – maybe," Pru spoke. "He could be a Coton de Tulear."

"Even better." Eleanor smiled, but it didn't reach her eyes. "Thank you, Pru. I think you're wasted here, but – oh, well."

"Oh, well?" Martha's eyes narrowed. "You're not selling my Teddy!"

"Ruff!"

"Wait a minute," Pru said slowly, "that was you this morning, walking past the café when I was speaking to Jesse."

"Very good. When I overheard you mention the case, I had to find out just how much you knew, so when I spotted your car parked outside that house this afternoon, I wrote the note and put it on your windshield.

"Now, let's get down to business. I'll take Teddy after I dispose of you. Two bumbling sleuths snooping where they shouldn't be, and don't

228

you know it? They have a fatal accident."

"That won't be happening." Pru squared her shoulders. "I'm calling Mitch right now."

"Yeah!" Martha waved her phone in the air. "My phone is switched on now, too."

"No, it's not." Eleanor plucked it out of Marth's hand and threw it toward the red maple trees.

"Hey! You can't do that!"

"But I just did." Eleanor smiled in satisfaction.

"Ruff!" Teddy scampered after the phone, the leash slipping from Pru's hand.

"Teddy!" She started after him, her eyes widening when she spotted the bucket of water nearby. Snatching it up, she crept behind Eleanor, who was still threatening Martha, and threw the water over her head.

"Arggh!" Eleanor's hands flapped around, feeling her wet hair.

"Run, Martha!" Pru shouted. "I'll get Teddy!"

"Ruff!" Teddy bounded over to Martha, her phone in his mouth.

"Good boy." Martha scooped him up and placed him in the walker basket. "But we've gotta hurry!"

Pru raced after Martha and Teddy and bundled them into the car, aware that Eleanor had recovered from her soaking, and was running after them.

She gunned the engine and squealed out of the parking lot, leaving Martha's walker standing in the dust of the exhaust fumes.

"I guess your brothers taught you some useful stuff," Martha commented. "Like getting away from a bad guy – or gal."

"They taught me to drive." Pru laughed in reaction. "Including how to get out of a place in a hurry. I never thought it would come in handy, though."

Martha turned her head and looked back at the library. "Eleanor's stomping her feet – I hope she doesn't take her bad mood out on my walker. I really do love that thing, even if I grumble about it sometimes."

"Ruff!"

EPILOGUE

Two days later, Mitch stopped by Martha's house late afternoon. Pru had just gotten off work, and was relaxing in the living room with Martha and Teddy.

After they'd escaped Eleanor, Pru drove them straight to the police station, where they'd detailed their encounter with her.

Mitch had taken action immediately, and had nabbed Eleanor on the street outside the library as she'd started her aging BMW.

"These are for you." Mitch held out a cardboard box. "It's Lauren's day off, but when she heard about what happened, she thought you might need some freshly baked cupcakes."

"Goody!" Martha's eyes lit up and she opened the box. "Ooh – carrot cake. And look at all that frosting!"

Pru's mouth watered at the sight of the high swirls of cream cheese frosting on the six cupcakes.

"Ruff?" Teddy rose on his hind legs and tried to peer into the box.

"I already gave you an extra doggy treat yesterday and today," Martha told him, "for being such a good boy for fetching my phone after Eleanor threw it away." She turned to Mitch. "It still works!"

"That's good." Mitch smiled.

"Would you like some coffee?" Pru offered. "I think we've got some juice as well."

"Thanks, but I'm good. I just wanted to update you about Eleanor. She'll be going away for a while – she confessed everything after I arrested her, with her lawyer present. And I've brought back your walker. I'll just get it."

"Thanks," Martha said. "It's been a bit strange without it, but I've been able to manage."

Mitch strode to the front door and wheeled in the rolling walker.

"Here you go."

"I've had it for a while now, so I think it's become part of me." Martha stroked one of the handles. "It looks the same as it did on Saturday – goody. Eleanor didn't do anything to it."

"We checked it over at the station and couldn't see any signs of tampering," Mitch informed her.

"Thank you," Pru said.

"So, after finding your first murder victim, are you going to stick around Gold Leaf Valley?" he asked. "It's a pretty safe town, apart from the occasional murder."

Martha and Teddy looked at her hopefully.

"You betcha!" Pru smiled.

"Ruff!"

THE END

I hope you enjoyed reading this mystery.

If you sign up to my newsletter, you'll receive a Free and Exclusive short story titled **When Martha Met Her**

Match. It's about Martha adopting Teddy from the animal shelter and takes place during **Prowling at the Premiere – A Norwegian Forest Cat Café Cozy Mystery – Book 23**, but it can also be read as a standalone, and it's also the first title in Martha's Senior Sleuthing Club series. I decided Martha and Teddy should have their own series!

Sign up to my newsletter here:
www.JintyJames.com

If you already receive my newsletter and didn't receive the short story, please email at **jinty@jintyjames.com** with the email address you used to sign up with, and I'll send you the link.

Please turn the page for a list of all my books – have you missed any?

TITLES BY JINTY JAMES

Purrs and Peril – A Norwegian Forest Cat Café Cozy Mystery – Book 1

Meow Means Murder - A Norwegian Forest Cat Café Cozy Mystery – Book 2

Whiskers and Warrants - A Norwegian Forest Cat Café Cozy Mystery – Book 3

Two Tailed Trouble – A Norwegian Forest Cat Cafe Cozy Mystery – Book 4

Paws and Punishment – A Norwegian Forest Cat Café Cozy Mystery – Book 5

Kitty Cats and Crime – A Norwegian Forest Cat Café Cozy Mystery – Book 6

Catnaps and Clues - A Norwegian
Forest Cat Café Cozy Mystery – Book
7

Pedigrees and Poison – A Norwegian
Forest Cat Café Cozy Mystery – Book
8

Christmas Claws – A Norwegian
Forest Cat Café Cozy Mystery – Book
9

Fur and Felons - A Norwegian Forest
Cat Café Cozy Mystery – Book 10

Catmint and Crooks – A Norwegian
Forest Cat Café Cozy Mystery – Book
11

Kittens and Killers – A Norwegian
Forest Cat Café Cozy Mystery – Book
12

Felines and Footprints – A Norwegian
Forest Cat Café Cozy Mystery – Book
13

Catnip and Capture – A Norwegian Forest Cat Café Cozy Mystery – Book 21

Mice and Malice – A Norwegian Forest Cat Café Cozy Mystery – Book 22

Prowling at the Premiere – A Norwegian Forest Cat Café Cozy Mystery – Book 23 (Teddy appears for the first time in this book.)

Maddie Goodwell Series (fun witch cozies)

Spells and Spiced Latte - A Coffee Witch Cozy Mystery - Maddie Goodwell 1 – Free!

Visions and Vanilla Cappuccino - A Coffee Witch Cozy Mystery - Maddie Goodwell 2

Magic and Mocha – A Coffee Witch Cozy Mystery – Maddie Goodwell 3

Enchantments and Espresso – A
Coffee Witch Cozy Mystery – Maddie
Goodwell 4

Familiars and French Roast - A
Coffee Witch Cozy Mystery – Maddie
Goodwell 5

Incantations and Iced Coffee – A
Coffee Witch Cozy Mystery – Maddie
Goodwell 6